I0788377

Sherrilyn's Worlds

A PICTOGRAPHIC HISTORY OF HER MULTIPLE
#1 BESTSELLING SERIES

Madaug & Ian Kenyon

Nemesis Press
Franklin, TN

To our mom

*Sometimes you have to put your foot down . . .
Sometimes you have to put it up their asses.*

—Hauk, Born of Fury

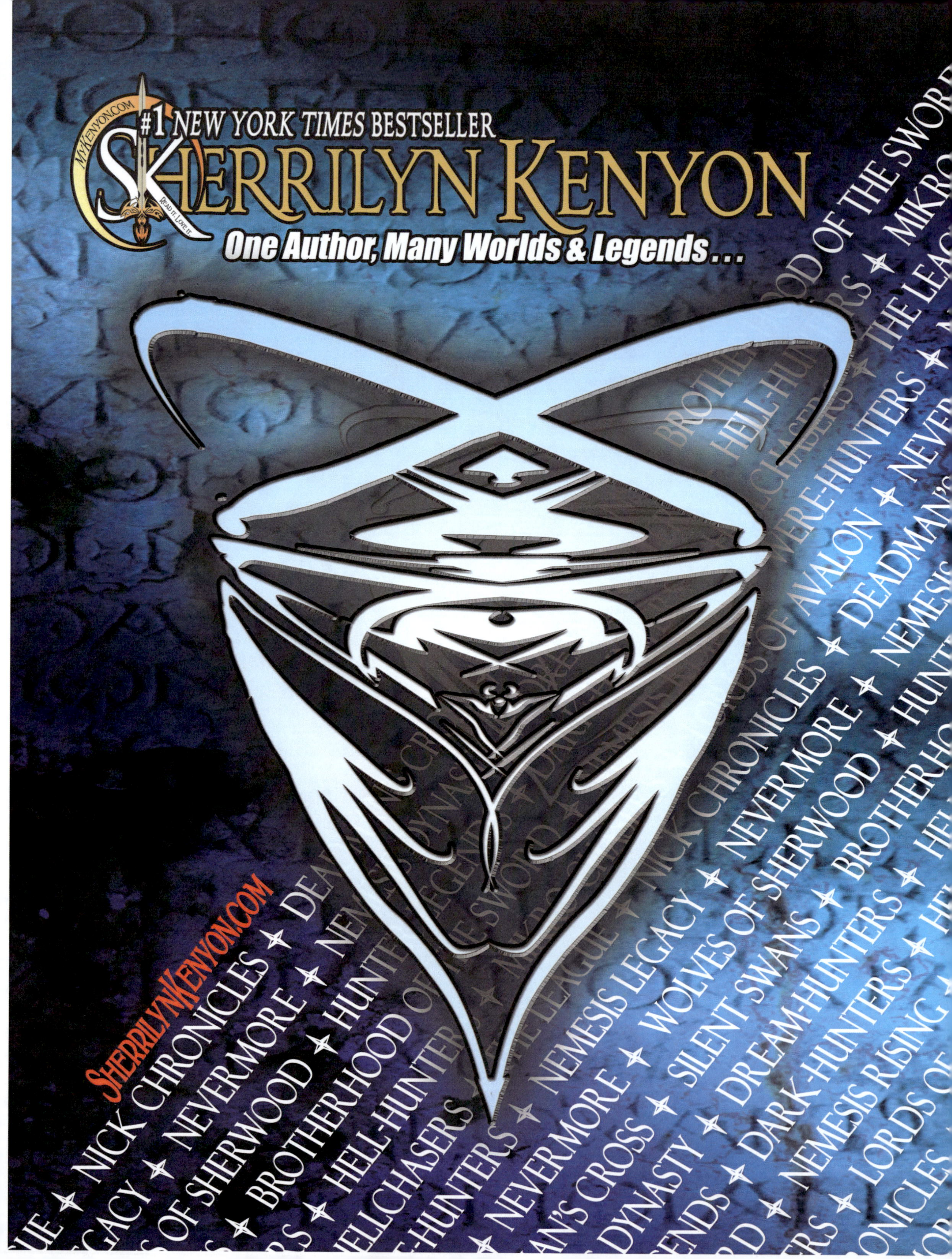

MyKenyon.com
READ IT. LOVE IT.
#1 NEW YORK TIMES BESTSELLER
SHERRILYN KENYON
One Author, Many Worlds & Legends . . .
SherrilynKenyon.com

Forward

I first began writing as soon as I could hold a crayon in my hand. Before I knew what words were on a page, I was telling stories with pictures. I'd draw them and then run off to my parents or siblings (or my dolls and stuffed animals whenever my family became bored listening to me) and tell them all about the adventures I'd created in my head. Many times, I've tried to think back and figure out what first started those voices, to no avail. They've always been there. I can't imagine a life where I didn't hear Nykyrian or Acheron, or any of the thousands of others who share my mind with me. Never once have I been alone. My whole life has been an endless struggle to write down as much about them as I could as fast as I could.

The number one question fans and interviewers ask me is if I ever thought my series, any of them, would become as popular as they have. I've always been honest. I'm a writer, first and foremost, which means I have an active and wild imagination. As a young girl, I thought I'd be queen of the universe. I saw it clearly in my mind. But in reality, I never really considered outside people embracing the worlds I was making up. Yes, I wanted to be published. I craved it horribly. I've always wanted everyone to love my people as much as I do. It was why I talked to everything, including the bedpost about them. However, my number one priority has been to the people who live in my head and heart. To do the best that I can with the stories they give me and hope that maybe, just maybe, I can entertain others as much as those stories entertain me.

What that means is that I measure success by the smiles of my readers and the hugs they give when we meet. That was why I got into this business. Books saved my life. When I was a child and trapped in a horrible past that I try my best never to look back on, those characters and worlds created by others allowed me to learn that what I was living wasn't normal and that there could be a better existence outside the hell I knew. They taught me to look forward and not focus on things that couldn't be changed or to be bogged down by those determined to keep me mired in the misery they'd created for me. Those authors and books kept me sane and saved me. I owe them everything and that is a debt I want to pay forward. That is why I wrote then and why I write today.

So many times in my life, those books and characters were the only friends or hope I had. They saw me through my darkest hours and worst nightmares. I've wished a million times that the world was a better place for everyone. That no one would ever know the sad places that exist to drag us down from our dreams and happiness. That no child knew fear in their home. No human went to bed at night wishing they wouldn't wake up in the morning.

What a beautiful world this would be if people put as much energy into lifting others up as they did into tearing each other down. Yet in spite of everything I've seen and been through, I still manage to hold on to that shred of hope because I refuse to let the darkness take me and make me a part of it. I will not let it consume me.

I will do better. For the sake of my boys and for the sake of my characters, and for those who are out there like I've been so many times in my life who need that little bit of light in the storm to guide them to a safe harbor where maybe, just maybe they can have a moment's worth of peace. Because I do believe in the impossible. It's what allows me to write about military assassins who fly across galaxies and demons who fight for the good of mankind. Because I hope that in the end good will win out and that somehow justice will be served.

Most of all, I believe in second chances, even when they seem impossible. Even when we're on the ground and we've been kicked so many times that we don't know how to get back up, I believe in staggering back to my feet to rise to a new challenge. Because I saw my mother rise up when she had no reason to and every reason to quit. And I know that I am all my sons have in this world. If nothing else, I owe it to them and to my readers and characters to give this world all I have, even when I have nothing left but that tiny little sliver of hope.

If you're new to my worlds, I hope you'll give them a try. I write a little of everything. I was never the type to let labels define me. That defiance gave me a lot of trouble in the early days of my career as I refused to stick to any one genre. Some days, it still does. But I think life is what we make it, and if there's something we want we should let nothing stop us from going after it. Over, under, around or through. We can all achieve our dreams. Even those elusive ones that seem impossible.

Just like the doctors who told my mother that my Cerebral Palsy sister would never walk. Though it took my mother eight years, she taught Patricia to walk and Trish walks to this day. As mom my used to say, sometimes impossible just means you have to try a little harder.

For my fans, I hope you enjoy this little trip into the past and future that my boys put together for you. Some of the art you've probably seen before. Some of it, the boys found in forgotten files. It was a fun project for them, I think. And hopefully we'll meet soon at an event!

Hugs always,

YOU DON'T KNOW STYXX!
DARK-HUNTER.COM

STYXX WAS FRAMED!

L
VE
Στύγιος ομάδα

ἀλέξω

YOU DON'T KNOW STYXX!

Sibling Rivalry

Since the beginning of time, Kadar and Shyamala have been scheming against the rest of their siblings. No one is quite sure why Shyamala decided to change her name to Azura, but we're sure that one day soon the answer will be known. While Azura keeps herself in the background, Kadar (Noir) is always out front, torturing all those around him. Especially now that the Malachai has escaped and he wants him back.

The war of the original seven siblings is what gives us the backdrop of the Dark-Hunters universe.

The Seven Are:

1. *Braith*
2. *Cam*
3. *Azura*
4. *Rezar*
5. *Kadar*
6. *Verlyn*
7. *Lilith*

Of course, we can't give any spoilers, but suffice it to say, Braith (shown here) becomes our beloved goddess of destruction and the mother of our series (after Sherrilyn).

The Rivalry

Never one to be outdone by her evil sisters or brother, Cam was the goddess who conceived the idea of creating an army of Sephirii to help protect the innocent from the demons and other preternaturals who preyed on them. Fierce warriors who were supposed to keep Kadar, Azura and Braith (Apollymi) in line, the Sephirii didn't draw their powers from the main Source, but rather from conflict—something that made them an unstoppable force in battle, even against the gods. However, Rezar and Verlyn quickly saw the danger in that and made sure they brought them under subjugation to them.

Cam didn't argue. As the original goddess of balance and justice, she thought it her duty to help maintain a balance between the gods and the mortal species. Little did she know, she was paving the way for the bloodiest battle of all.

As we learn in later books, Cam becomes Menyara as she's shown here. She's not only a guiding force in the Nick Chronicles, but is one of the key players in the Deadman's Cross series as well.

More Sibling Rivalry

Since the beginning of time, Kadar and Shyamala have been scheming against the rest of their siblings. No one is quite sure why Shyamala decided to change her name to Azura, but we're sure that one day soon the answer will be known. While Azura keeps herself in the background, Kadar (Noir) is always out front, torturing all those around him. Especially now that the Malachai has escaped and he wants him back.

The war of the original seven siblings is what gives us the backdrop of the Hunter Legends universe that includes: the Dark-Hunters, Were-Hunters, Dream-Hunters, Hellchasers, Chronicles of Nick, Deadman's Cross, Lords of Avalon and MikroChasers.

Weakened without the Malachai, Noir and Azura are trapped in Azmodea where they plot against humanity and await the day when they'll be free again.

Apollymi's Symbol

While Braith's/Apollymi's symbol was that of a sun, once she invited Stryker and his Spathi into her domain, her symbol changed to that with a dragon coiled through her sun emblem to represent their alliance against Apollo. They use this symbol to this day.

Enter Kissare

In defiance to the gods and his orders, the leader of the Sephirii fell in love with the goddess he served (Braith) and had an illicit affair with her. Married in secret, they would become the parents of a new race of demons that would rise up to compete with the Sephirii in powers and battle skills.

For his love, Kissare was sentenced to death. But he made a promise to Apollymi (his nickname for Braith) that he would defy death itself to come back for her and their son.

The Malachai Rises

Monakribos, the son of Apollymi and Kissare, is a force to be reckoned with. From the moment Monakribos enters this world, Kadar and Azura see the potential and use his blood to create a counter race to the Sephirii. The Malachai demons. Because the Malachai are a mixture of pure evil and good who draw their powers from the Source and from conflict and fighting, they quickly become the most powerful creatures in existence (aside from the gods), and it's not long before war breaks out between the contentious gods and their "children."

For his love, Kissare was sentenced to death. But he made a promise to Apollymi that he would defy death itself to come back for her and their son.

Jaden's Emblem

Official Dream-Hunters Emblem

Angry Gods

Verlyn becomes one of the strongest warriors for the Kalosum. His powers are so great that Kadar and Azura quickly realize he must be controlled. In an effort to do so, Azura seduces him and tries the oldest way in history to exert her will over him—she births him a son.

Like the Malachai emblem, Jaden's symbol is one Sherri created in college. Having grown up as an Army brat, she was fascinated by military patches and used to collect them. It was only natural for her to begin designing her own for her characters as far back as childhood. Jaden's "mask" symbol is actually made out of crossed angel wings. If you look at the Dream-Hunters' shield, you can see her original hand-drawn marks.

Caleb Malphas

The son of Verlyn/Jaden and a demon, Malphas is torn between his two warring natures and is rejected by both parents. Like his half-brother, Xevikan whose mother is Azura, he is outcast by the Kalosum. While Jaden loves his sons, he can't trust them due to the fact that their mothers tricked him and continue to use them as weapons against him.

Both sons end up playing critical roles in the Primus Bellum, and in the centuries to come. Xevikan is first enslaved to the original Malachai bloodline to be their blood king, while Malphas ends up later enslaved to Adarian Malachai.

A Daeva demon, Caleb is able to assume many forms. But when human, he favors his father, with black hair. As a demon, his eyes are yellow.

Jared

Told that he's a son of Verlyn and the Sephiroth Myone, Jared grows up to become one of the strongest Sephirii warriors and takes his mother's place as their leader. During the Primus Bellum, he became a key player and made a decision to save his "father's" life that had horrific repercussions for him for the rest of time.

THE LAST SEPHIROTH

Because of his curse, Jared becomes the last of his kind and his life is forever tied to that of the last Malachai. Forbidden to die, he will spend eternity paying for a bargain he would give anything to take back. However, he also holds the key to the survival of all life as we know it.

Chthonians

It's during the Primus Bellum—First War—that the Chthonians are created to protect the new, burgeoning human species and keep us all from dying out as the gods war against each other. Because they don't play well with others, and are immortals born to protect mortals with the powers to kill the gods, they divide the world up between themselves and don't mingle with each other.

SAVITAR

And yep, this is when everyone's favorite surfer comes in to play. Born on the mysterious island of Mur or Lemuria as most know it, he is a creature of many, many secrets, and very few shirts and shoes.

SYMBOL OF
ARCHON KOSMETAS

ATLANTEAN GOD OF ORDER

After the War

The gods go their separate ways. Having lost both her husband and child, Apollymi is told that Archon is her beloved Kissare returned to her—a promise he made before the Kalosum executed him. So she settles in Atlantis to become their primary goddess and the queen of their pantheon. For centuries, she is happy, even though she is the goddess of destruction. Her only sadness comes from the fact that she never has another child of her own.

Archon tricks Apollymi and while she is faithful to him, he doesn't return the favor.

Apollymi of Atlantis

To end the war, the Kalosum had demanded the life of Apollymi's only child, Monakribos. Devastated by their cruelty, she turns her back on all her siblings and transforms herself into the ice-cold goddess of destruction we know and love. She refuses to have anything to do with her brothers or sisters ever again.

In Atlantis, she does her best to make a new home and forget about the drama she left behind.

The Apollymi shown here is treasuring her rare time with her grandkids. Since we don't want to give too many spoilers, all we can say is, read the series . . .

Grim Reaper

One of the most vicious curses placed on the Malachai came from Kadar's son-in-law, Mot, or Grim as he's better known.

KIRAST KIROZA KIRENT

Conceived in violence to do violence and to die violently. That means that every Malachai born (there can only be one at a time) will die by the hand of his own son once his son reaches puberty. Needless to say, no Malachai likes Grim very much.

A New Chance

After centuries of trying to have a child with Archon, Apollymi finally awakens to the news she's been waiting for. Yet when she goes to tell her husband, he doesn't share her joy.

A New Nightmare

Archon's three daughters who grow up to become the Fates in Greece are immediately terrified by Apollymi's news as they know how the goddess is when it comes to what she holds dear. Distressed, the little girls speak without thought and proclaim that her unborn child will be the end of them all. Since they're holding hands, their words are binding. And damning as the minute Archon and the others hear it, they decide that the only way to circumvent their destruction is to murder Apollymi's unborn son.

Apollymi refuses. She cuts her child prematurely from her womb and hides him in the belly of a human queen to raise as her own. Her punishment is to be imprisoned until she tells them where her son is or he dies.

Acheron & Styxx

Uniting her son's life to that of an innocent's has some unexpected repercussions. For all of them. Especially since Styxx isn't exactly a normal kid, either. Trying to avoid prophecy isn't all it's cracked up to be. And things never go quite as planned. As Apollymi says, the gift of foresight, isn't one of her powers.

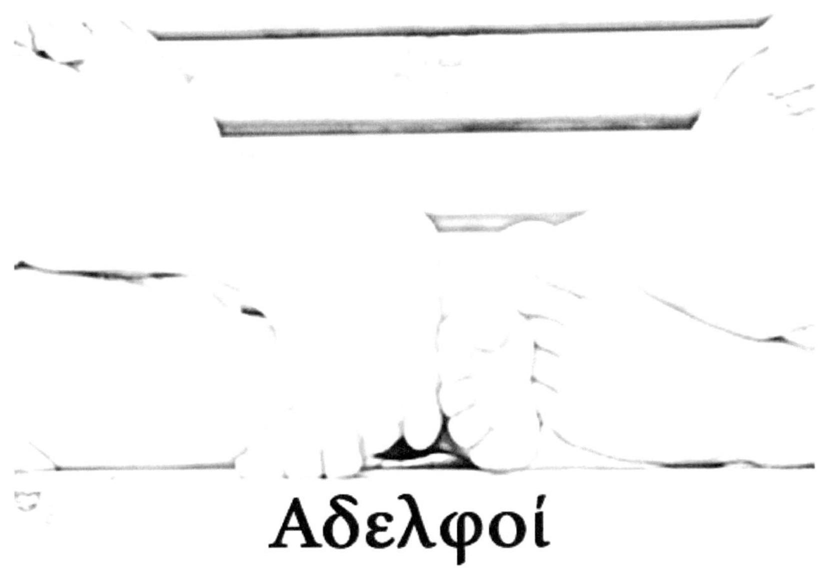

The twins are shown here in their true forms . . .

Acheron Parthenopaeus

Born into the body of a mortal, Acheron was never meant to be human. He is a god who grows up unwanted, and yet becomes a natural protector for mankind against the preternatural predators out to end us all.

Official ® Acheron Emblem

Under the Protection of

ACHERON

YEAROFACHERON.COM

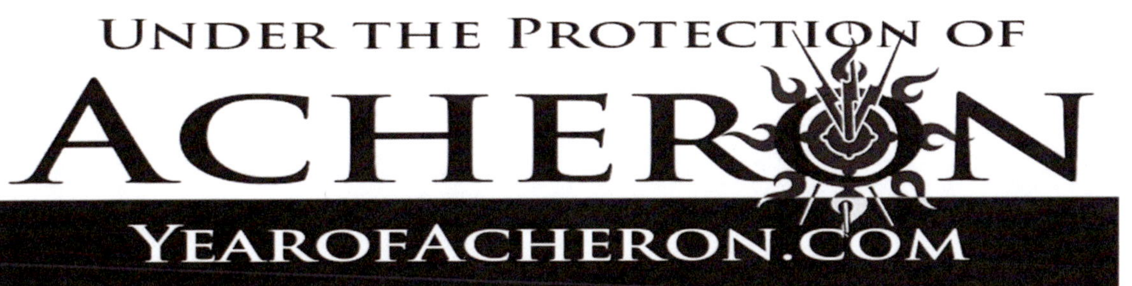

Acheron Parthenopaeus

A creature of many facets and faces, Ash is hard to get to know. He's either your best friend or worst nightmare.

Ryssa of Didymos

Braving her father's wrath, Ryssa "kidnaps" Acheron from their uncle's custody and takes him to their summer palace where she can care for him, giving him a respite from the nightmare of his life.

Acheron Parthenopaeus

Ryssa becomes Acheron's self-proclaimed protector. But there's only so much she can do. Every day they're together is one where she risks her own life for his.

Acheron Parthenopaeus

But their peace doesn't last. All too soon, Acheron is returned to the horror that is his uncle's house and Ryssa is left to hate and blame Styxx for Acheron's fate, even though Styxx is in no better shape and is unable to do anything to help him or himself.

Kalosis

Meanwhile, Apollymi sits imprisoned in the Atlantean hell realm, Kalosis, where she is unable to see or do anything to help her son. All she can do is whisper out to him to remain hidden and stay away from the gods who are out to kill him.

Styxx of Didymos

Meanwhile, Styxx is being trained for war and is expected to lead his people against Atlantis in battle. Alone and mocked, Styxx yearns for the days when he and Acheron weren't at each other's throats, but nothing can rectify the damage that their family has done to them.

Styxx of Didymos

While Ryssa loves Acheron, Styxx has only her animosity. There's nothing he can do to please her other than die and that's the one thing he's not willing to do.

Styxx of Didymos

In spite of his family's disdain and his young age, Styxx emerges as one of the greatest military leaders of the ancient world. His Stygian Omada becomes the stuff of legends.

STYXX
DARK-HUNTER

Styxx & Bethany

When he least expects it, Styxx stumbles across what he believes is a young, peasant girl fishing. Little does he know that the girl he falls in love with is actually an Egyptian and Atlantean goddess that he will spend the rest of eternity devoted to, and one who will alter his life forever. But not before she almost gets him killed as he has sworn to defeat her pantheon that he is currently at war with.

Styxx of Didymos

Once the war ends with Atlantis, Styxx spends time imprisoned there after the god Apollo vindictively makes a present of him to the gods he defeated. Forced to compete to stay alive, Styxx barely survives. It's a lesson about people and the gods that he never forgets.

Artemis

Artemis

Just when things can get no worse for the twins, enter the goddess Artemis who decides that she needs a piece of Ash . . . and that she can't live without him. She will spend the rest of eternity pursuing everyone's favorite Atlantean god and making him miserable.

Acheron the Harbinger

But on their twenty-first birthday, everything changes. Acheron receives his powers from his mother and he is no longer just a pawn to the world he hates. He is now an Atlantean god bent on vengeance against those who have done him wrong.

DARK-HUNTER

#1 NEW YORK TIMES BESTSELLING AUTHOR
SHERRILYN KENYON
SHERRILYNKENYON.COM

Acheron the Unwanted

Though Artemis has tied Acheron to her, she refuses to acknowledge their relationship. She's ashamed of him and her refusal to accept him causes centuries of problems for the them both. Especially Acheron who cannot rid himself of the green-eyed monster who won't let him live in peace or free him from the slavery she's forced him into.

Styxx Anaxkolasi

In one night, Styxx loses everything he ever knew. Atlantis is sunk to the bottom of the sea and Didymos is wiped from the face of the earth. Apollymi kills his wife and child, and he is imprisoned in Hades where he will spend the next eleven thousand years plotting revenge against the world.

Acheron Enslaved

After being brutally murdered by Apollo in retaliation for the death of Ryssa and her son which Acheron had no part in, Acheron is brought back to life by Artemis who uses her blood to enslave him and tie him to her for eternity. He's not real happy about it.

Simi Parthenopaeus

Ash is given one unexpected gift on his return to life that isn't so bad . . . most days. His own little Charonte demon, Simi. Instead of using her as she was intended; a bodyguard, he adopts the demon as a daughter and spoils her mercilessly.

Acheron

Simi & Acheron

The two are inseparable. Acheron is completely devoted to his demon daughter and Simi won't be parted from her "akri."

Simi's ABCs

And for those wondering, these adorable images are from the bestselling Simi's ABCs. A fun romp that showcases Sherri's #1 bestselling Dark-Hunters® characters for her younger readers. The Dark-Hunters® aren't just novels written for adults. Sherri's massive world encompasses bestselling manga, comics, graphic novels, coloring books, as well as the Mikrochasers® that are comics and younger readers for children and the #1 international bestselling Nick Chronicles AKA Chronicles of Nick® for Young Adults.

Illarion

Alethea Kontis & The Dabel Bros

Sherri's friends, Alethea Kontis and the Dabel Brothers, joined her in the production of *Simi's ABCs*. Alethea was also the author of the 2007 *Dark-Hunters Companion*®, for which the Dabels provided original art. Some of the content in the Companion was from Sherri's Dark-Hunters® site that Sherrilyn designed and launched by herself in 1999. The website was the culmination of the notes, and some of the character profiles and short stories Sherri had written and published in the 1980s. It also featured the original Dark-Hunter® handbook that Sherri had designed and wrote while attending Georgia College. The original logos were drawn by Sherrilyn while she was an art student at Georgia College and the University of Georgia. Sherri's friend, Rickey Mallory aka Mallory Kane (another bestselling author) was the one who told Sherri she should put her art and handbook online for fans to reference as Rickey had been telling Sherri since 1991 that her world was so vast that readers would want a refresher between books as "the author's brain is not included," and that it would help her readers to see just how intricate and amazing (and well thought-out) every detail of the Dark-Hunters universe was.

Strykerius Apoulos

Acheron and Styxx weren't the only two "musical" babies back in they day. While Apollymi was busy hiding her son in the womb of a Greek queen, Apollo heard about the Atlantean god, Archon, going crazy and slaughtering infant sons in Atlantis in an effort to keep his pantheon alive. Since the Atlantean queen was currently pregnant with the Greek god's son and everyone knew that her husband had been long dead at the time of conception, he figured his son would be slaughtered on arrival. So, to keep Stryker alive, as well as his dream of overthrowing his own father one day, Apollo stole a random fetus and swapped it with his son and had Stryker raised in Greece by his priestesses.

The poor queen of Atlantis, Xura, is never told that her son with Apollo is safe and alive. She believes that the Atlantean god, Archon, has her infant killed at birth and that her former lover, Apollo does nothing to spare their son his fate. All she knows is that Apollo turned his back on her pleas for mercy and allowed their child to die at Archon's hands. It's that hatred that turns into a bitter jealousy when she learns about Ryssa in Greece and her affair with Apollo. The birth of their son is what causes Xura to send her men out to slaughter Ryssa and Apollodorus (Apollo's son).

By trying to avenge her child, Stryker, Xura unknowingly curses him and her own grandchildren to an early, horrible death and damns her entire race and kingdom for eternity.

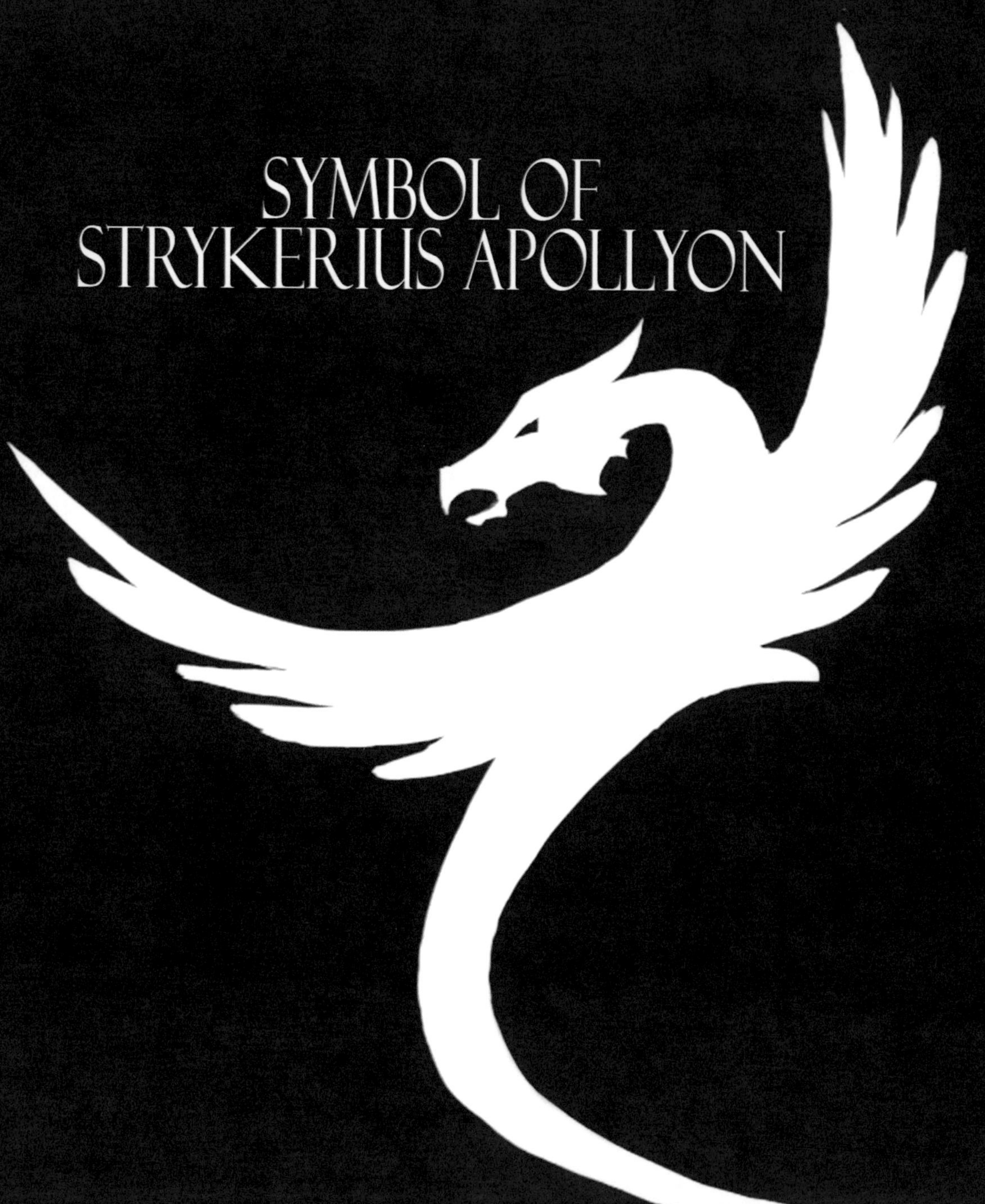

SYMBOL OF
STRYKERIUS APOLLYON

LEADER OF THE SPATHI DAIMONS

Strykerius Apollyon

While Apollymi adds a dragon to her sun emblem to show her unity with Stryker, Stryker removes the sun from his to show his break from his father, Apollo, the sun god. Once his father curses him and his children to die at the age of twenty-seven for something he had no part in, Stryker goes to his father's worst enemy, the Atlantean goddess, Apollymi and makes a bargain. She is the one who shows him how to circumvent his father's curse and to prey on the human race so that he and his people can take human souls and artificially elongate their lives past the short twenty-seven years they've been sentenced to. It's a high price, but one Stryker is willing to pay to see his children and people survive.

No longer Strykerius Apoulos (son of Apollo), he becomes Strykerius Apollyon—Stryker, son of Apollymi..

Urian Thánatago

There's also another secret Apollymi keeps about Stryker's son, Urian. One that will explain why he's stronger than his brothers, as well as why she brought the Apollites and Daimons into her domain. But since some of our readers might not have read Stygian yet, we'll leave that for you to uncover . . .

Just remember whenever you're reading Sherri's books, keep your eyes open to every detail. You never know what's important.

Rise of the Spathi

Once Stryker and his people move into Kalosis with Apollymi who is trapped there so long as Acheron lives, they begin to make a peculiar home and alliance. More and more Apollites join them and turn Daimon, and with them they discover all kinds of "fun" things. And some Spathi are a little harder to handle.

Desiderius

One such Spathi is Desiderius. A demigod with a bit of an attitude disorder who not only gives the Dark-Hunters a run for their money but gets a little lippy with Stryker and Urian. Something that is never a good idea . . . for anyone.

Urian Strykeros

Under their father's tutelage, Urian and his brothers quickly rise to become some of the greatest warriors in the ancient world. While they are unaware of Dark-Hunters at this time, they will go after anyone who threatens their people.

Dante's Inferno
The Serengeti Club
SANCTUARY
WERE-HUNTER.COM

Laminas & Limani

Apollites and Daimons begin to find ways to let each other know about their havens (lamani) in the human world where they can gather without fear of humans preying on them and where they'll be among their own kind. One such way is with banners and symbols the humans won't recognize, but that are innate to their species. They quickly adopt Stryker's former emblem as a way of designating such sanctuaries.

Yes, it galls Stryker, but he learns to live with it for the sake of his people.

A laminas, a Daimon or Apollite sanctuary, should never be confused with the many limani in the world, Were-Hunter sanctuaries. While those often honor the code of not killing Daimons, they don't all do so. And a laminas will never return the favor. If a Were-Hunter or Dark-Hunter shows up there, they become lunch. The Were-Hunters didn't think that through when they chose a name so close to the Daimons' bolt-holes.

First Dark-Hunters

For thousands of years, Acheron fights the Daimons alone and is doing a bang-up job of it. The only problem is that Artemis feels neglected. So to get his attention, she uses some of his powers to create a race of beings she knows he'll feel guilty about and uses it to manipulate him.

Like so many backbiting schemes, it doesn't work out the way she plans. Most people don't like to be manipulated by those who betrayed them, and Acheron is no exception. He agrees to train the warriors Artemis has created, but he's not happy about it.

Ias of Groesia

One of the first Dark-Hunters created, Ias is also the first to die. Unfortunately, Acheron learns some very harsh lessons about Artemis's new army and the extent of his own powers. At Ias's expense. But his death isn't in vain. Because of it, Acheron sets up ground rules with Artemis about what she'll provide for the Dark-Hunters she creates, and he forces her to give each one an out on the contract the Dark-Hunter makes with the goddess so that they can earn back their soul, and not be trapped the way Ias was.

Ias, though he is now a ghost dependent on Acheron's blood, is taken into Ash's home in the Atlantean heaven realm, Katateros, and allowed to live there so as not to be in chronic pain.

There, he becomes Ash's Alexion, a steward who oversees his home and helps with the care of Simi.

Squires

Originally called shield-bearers, the Squires are one of the compromises Acheron gets from Artemis. They are an organization of humans set up to help hide Dark-Hunters in the human world. Well-funded and kept in total secret, they are a shadow organization that will do whatever it takes to ensure that no one discovers the existence of the immortal warriors who keep us safe from the preternatural threats who stalk us. They have schools set up to train their children and are a world unto themselves. In time, they become their own shadow world, with secret operatives and organizations that run deep covert missions all over the globe.

Mad, Bad & Immortal

With Acheron now greeting and training all new Dark-Hunters, the DH and their Squires become a force to be reckoned with. Because Artemis wants to cement Acheron at her side, their numbers grow quickly, and they spread far and wide, to battle the Daimon menace. While Acheron is a reluctant wrangler, he settles into his role, even if it means having to keep Simi from eating the heifer-goddess and keeping his Dark-Hunters out of trouble.

Double Trouble

Yet Ash is a creature of many secrets and his past is never far from his mind. Neither is the reality that he has a twin brother capable of ruining him should anyone ever learn about Styxx and their relationship, or what Acheron has been through.

House of Didymos Emblem

Styxx Shield

Urian Shield

Secrets Abound

Styxx isn't the only secret in the Dark-Hunter world. There are many surprises hidden and Stryker has a few of his own. Not to mention, Styxx isn't what he seems, and he has his own story to tell. As he says to his brother, "just because you had it bad, it doesn't mean that I had it good."

The Dark-Hunters

But through it all, Acheron fights on and unites his Hunters. Better than anyone, he understands what's at stake and he has no intention of watching the world burn.

A Hero Among Gods

In spite of the hell that mankind put Acheron through, and all the horrors of Artemis, he still manages to hold onto a shred of his conscience. Not that it's always easy. And no, he doesn't always do the right thing for the right reasons—Styxx and Alexion are both living proofs of that, but Acheron does try his best and he does learn from his mistakes. At the end of the day, he is perfectly imperfect.

Were-Hunters

Born half-human, half-Apollite, we were stricken by the ancient gods and cast down out of jealousy. My great-grandfather sought to save us. To preserve us.

Out of his love and magic we, and our cousins, the Katagaria, were created.

Since we are born of two worlds, we walk of two worlds. Time and dimension have no meaning to us. We aren't bound by the laws of mortal physics. Mystical and mythical, we walk through dimensions and time, and even space itself--- finding our homes and peace wherever we can.

We are half animal, half human. Half demon and half saint. At war within ourselves and without.

A race of both wizards and barbarians, we are capable of extreme compassion and utter, cold-blooded ruthlessness.

We have been called many things by those who fear us: demons, witches, warlocks, sorcerers shape-shifters, even vampires and devils.

Pursued by our enemies and even by our own, we are the last great race of warriors.

House of Kattalakis

Kattalakis

Of the animals chosen to be Were-Hunters, Lycaon picks the two strongest to be bonded to his sons. Dragons and wolves. While not every wolf or dragon is descended from the princes, those who have blood ties are given the surname Kattalakis as a marker for the others to know that they are Were-Hunter royalty.

Dragonbane

The firstborn Katagaria dragon who killed the firstborn Arcadian dragon prince and heir so that he could become the Arcadian king and immortal. His actions started the blood war that lasts to this day. The Kattalakis Arcadian dragons have a bounty on his head of three hundred million dollars. The only problem is, no one knows what he looks like. They only know him by the royal seal that's branded onto his back.

Forever Divided

As part of their curse, the Were-Hunters are never supposed to marry across species. In fact, they have no choice in their spouses at all. The Fates assign them a mate, usually someone they can't stand and then they have to either accept the person the Fates have chosen for them, or they are left sterile for the rest of their lifetime. Another attempt of the gods to phase out their species.

Sometimes, however, the Were-Hunters defy the Fates and the gods. And interspecies mating isn't unheard of. Either in defiance or because the Fates themselves are just that cruel.

Twelve Branches

Lycaon experimented with many species, but not all survived. Of those that did, twelve are exist today. These are the groups that make up the current species of Were-Hunters.

- DRAKOS (Dragons)
- GERAKIAN (Falcon/Hawk)
- LYKOS (Wolves)
- NIPHETOS PARDALIA (Snow Leopard)
- PANTHIRAS (Panthers)
- PARDALIA (Leopard)
- TIGARIAN (Tigers)
- TSAKALI (Jackals)
- URSULAN (Bears)
- BALIOS (Jaguar)
- HELIKIAS (Cheetah)

Fang Kattalakis whose family is descended from the royal wolf branch, and Aimee Peltier whose bear family owns and runs the infamous Sanctuary bar & grill in New Orleans is one such couple in the series. They defy everyone, even the Fates to stay together.

Omegrion Council

The ruling council of the Were-Hunters. Similar to a senate, the Omegrion has one representative from each branch of the Arcadian and Katagaria that represents them all. They make laws that govern all the Were-Hunters and are responsible for setting up sanctuaries.

Answering directly to the Chthonian Savitar, they oversee and govern the Were-Hunters. And are made up of twenty-three members (twenty-four originally, but one species went extinct when they crossed the big guy in charge).

The Members Are

Or at least at the time of *Unleash the Night* because we don't want to give spoilers they were:

- Litarian (lions) - Patrice Leonides (A) Paris Sebastienne (K)
- Drakos (dragons) - Damos Kattalakis (A) Darion Kattalakis (K)
- Gerakian (hawks, falcons, and eagles) - Arion Petrakis (A) Draven Hawke (K)
- Tigarian (tigers) - Adrian Gavril (A) Lysander Stephanos (K)
- Lykos (wolves) - Vane Kattalakis (A) Fury Kattalakis (K)
- Ursulan (bears) - Leo Apollonian (A) Nicolette Peltier (K)
- Panthiras (panthers) - Alexander James (A) Dante Pontis (K)
- Tsakalis (jackals) - Constantine (A) Vincenzo Moretti (K)
- Niphetos Pardalia (snow leopards) - Anelise Romano (A) Wren Tigarian (K)
- Pardalia (leopards) - Dorian Kontis (A) Stefan Kouris (K)
- Balios (jaguars) - extinct (A) Myles Stephanopoulos (K)
- Helikias (cheetahs) - Jace Wilder (A) Michael Giovanni (K)

Apollite Cousins

While they might war among themselves, the Were-Hunters have never forgotten that they originated from the Apollites. And that they owe their magical powers, even their ability to time-travel, to the fact that they started out as kin to Apollo's pet race. As such, many of them will protect their Apollite and Daimon cousins from the Dark-Hunters who pursue them.

Dragonmark

They absorb power from the gods and can use it to attack. It makes them stronger and harder to kill than their counterparts. There's a prophecy that anyone who can command a Dragonmark in his army will never be defeated. Not by man. And never by the gods.

Dream-Hunters

Sired by the gods of sleep, nightmares and dreams, we are the children of Mist (and at times human mothers). All of us are born of the sacred, chosen bloodline.

Traditionally called the Oneroi, we are what protect the humans, Apollites, and immortals while they slumber. We are the Dream Warriors. The ones who battle the Skoti Daimons and demons who prey on the dreams and emotions of sleepers.

During the light of day, we walk among the humans as unknown phantoms. And whenever human eyes happen upon us, they immediately glance away without registering our presence (unless we will it otherwise).

Most of us are devoid of emotions (except for pain which is a physical response). Those who have been cursed to no emotions can only feel while in a dream state with a human or immortal host. But therein lies the danger–some of us come to crave emotions like a drug.

Instead of being observers and protectors, they become dream instigators- controllers of the host. They return over and over, manifesting the dreamers worst fears and horrors in an effort to create more intense emotions so that they can get a greater high. Should the evil Skotos continue to drain his/her victim, madness will descend and kill them. Hence the creation of a Dream-Hunter. Certain members of the Oneroi have been chosen to patrol the Skoti, and ensure they do not prey upon those who sleep.

The Dream-Hunters actually predate the Dark-Hunters. Sherri wrote her first "Oneroi" story when she was in high school. V'Aiden's story was originally sold to her school friends for twenty cents a copy. It would be years later, after she started writing Dark-Hunters that she'd bring them into the official "Hunter Legends" universe to be another branch that would heal the Dark-Hunters whenever they were sleeping and who could aid the DH in another realm to battle another form of villain.

Pyramid of Protection

Even though they are related to the Daimons and Apollites, the Were-Hunters do work with the Dark-Hunters and Dream-Hunters to protect humans from the creatures who prey upon them. Together, they provide a pyramid of protection that keeps all creatures safe from the things to go bump in the night.

Sanctuaries

In their quest to maintain peace and order, many Were-Hunters are keepers of havens that operate under Savitar's laws that are very basic: Come in peace or leave in pieces. Like the Dark-Hunters, they live in plain sight, but are never seen. A number of the Were-Hunter clans own bars and clubs that cater to humans and preternaturals alike. So the next time you go dancing or venture into a bar, look around, especially if the servers or staff are a little more handsome than normal. You just never know . . .

The Sanctuary motto: Come in peace, or leave in pieces, comes from Sherri's older brother who was once a bouncer. That was favorite saying to tell anyone entering a bar where he worked the door. Though he died January 21, 1987, Sherri has immortalized his words in her books as a tribute to him.

The Beginning

Fans meet the first Dark-Hunters in *Night Pleasures*, when Amanda Devereaux wakes up handcuffed to Kyrian of Thrace after Desiderius captures them both. The book took the world by storm, but it was a tough sell for Sherrilyn who first conceived the series in 1984 when she began it as short stories and the rough draft of over two dozen of the original first novels while attending Georgia College in Milledgeville, Georgia. The original characters and the world of the Dark-Hunters were started before Anne Rice had published her second novel, and years before *The Lost Boys* movie; more than a decade before *Buffy the Vampire Slayer*.

The whole reason Sherri called her villains Daimons instead of vampires was because no editor in New York would even consider a vampire novel for publication. They firmly believed that there was no market for such a book and that no audience existed for any kind of paranormal series.

Thirty-five years, over a hundred short stories, and with more than sixty-five Dark-Hunter books that have landed on hundreds of lists with multitudinous #1 bestsellers, Sherri has more than proved them wrong.

Tabitha Devereaux

In the first draft of *Night Pleasures* from the 1980's, Sherri had Tabitha matched with Kyrian, but no matter how hard she tried, Tabitha wouldn't stop trying to kill him. It wasn't until Sherri had the epiphany that she had the twins paired with the wrong Hunters that the books began to fall into place.

Tabby's Birth

The idea for Tabby was born from Sherri's early childhood and her mother's addiction to *Hammer Horror* films. As a girl, Sherri would pretend to be the vampire slayer and so when she went to write the stories as a teenager, she naturally wrote what she knew. A strong Goth female out to protect her friends and the world.

Sherrilyn first met Rickey Mallory AKA Mallory Kane when she was twenty-five years old. Rickey is the first person who will tell anyone of how many manuscripts and stories Sherri already had written and planned for the Dark-Hunters as early as 1991. The original novels up to **Unleash the Night** *were all conceived and drafted before Sherrilyn married her ex-husband. The photo below shows the apartment where she lived in Richmond, VA in 1991. You can see the pile of manuscripts she already had prepared and written that she was submitting to no avail.*

Selena Devereaux Laurens

Tabitha's sister, Selena appears in the opening scenes of the first two books as a bridge character. The Devereauxs have deep roots throughout the series and play integral parts. For those who've been keeping up with the Deadman's Cross trilogy, you've even met their ancestors, Sancha Dolorosa and Jake Devereaux, along with their cousin Jo's great-great-great-great-grandfather Blake ap Landrey. They're all members of Captain Bane's crew. Which is also why Tabitha, Amanda, and Selena, along with Tiyana, have the powers that they do. Like many other entities in the DH series, the sisters are more than they seem and you need to keep your eyes pealed while reading.

Selena's tarot stand is the same place where Sherri once read cards while she lived in New Orleans. Yes, it's true, Sherrilyn was a professional tarot card reader and was even licensed as such. Selena's nickname, the Moon Mistress, pays homage to Sherrilyn's old pseudonym she published some of the original short stories under: Cherice Moon. And that's how Nick's mom also gained her name.

Nick Gautier

While Nick, along with Tabby, Simi and many other characters made his original appearance in the Dark-Hunter short stories, most remember his first appearance as the iconic phone call with Kyrian while Kyrian is in the hospital during the scene in *Night Pleasures*. Our little Squire is quite the handful from the get-go. After all, only Nick would be brave or stupid enough to try and handle Zarek without a chaperone.

Of course, in the beginning, we all assume that's just because he's Cajun and reckless, right?

Nick takes his name from Gautier, Mississippi. A small town where Sherri used to stop for gas when she'd make the drive from New Orleans to Atlanta back in the 1980s.

Talon of the Morrigantes

An ancient Celtic warrior, Talon is one of Sherri's original characters from the 1980s short stories. Back in the day, Sherri used him as one of her D&D characters that she role-played and wrote about in high school. When she decided to write the Dark-Hunters, he was one of the first characters she wanted to populate their world with. While he was an ex-chieftain mercenary in her fantasy novels, his character remained virtually unchanged in Dark-Hunters. You'll also recognize his companion he had back in the day.

Simi, however, had a bigger transformation when she entered the Dark-Hunters universe.

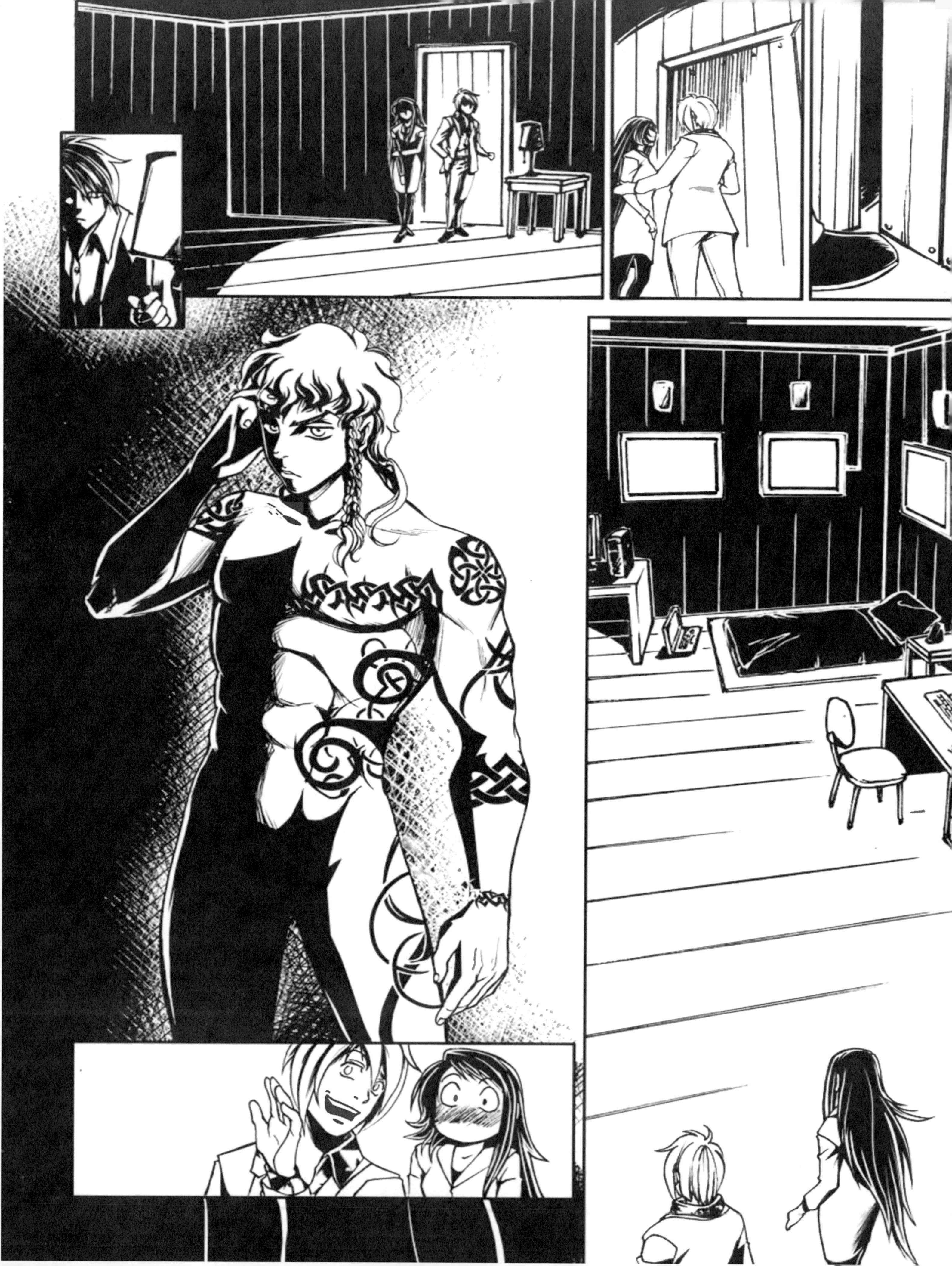

Night Embrace

Night Embrace was originally the size of the *Acheron* novel, but because the series was still considered unproven even though the first two books sold out as soon as they hit bookstore shelves and the publisher couldn't keep up with the demand, St. Martin's refused to publish the book in its entirety. Over two hundred pages were cut out of the book, including numerous scenes with the Were-Hunters. Some of those scenes appear in later books.

Ironically, Sherri wrote the book twice. Sections of the book were written in the 1980s and Sherri had some of them published as short stories. One of those original Dark-Hunters short stories was actually turned down by Marion Zimmer Bradley, three times, for her *Fantasy* magazine.

Even though **Night Pleasures** *hit an overall Amazon store ranking of #6, it would take St. Martin's years before they'd fully be on board with the series. Sherri was left to build her career and readership on her own while raising her three small sons. At one infamous meeting with her publisher right before the book came out, he asked Sherrilyn where she'd thought she'd be in five years. Sherri corageously said that she'd be on the* **New York Times** *list. Her publisher laughed in her face and told her not to get her hopes up.* **Night Embrace** *and* **Night Pleasures** *listed on the* **USA Today** *bestseller list just a few weeks after that. The next book,* **Kiss of the Night**, *landed in the top ten of the* **NYT**. *In less than five years of that conversation, Sherrilyn had multiple Dark-Hunter novels landing routinely at #1 on the* **New York Times** *list, thanks to her diligent hard work and her dedicated fans.*

Accidental Time Warp

Because there was no market or genre for paranormal at the time St. Martin's bought the Dark-Hunters and no other author or house was publishing that genre, St. Martin's took their time bringing out the first books after the offer was made (even though they had the finished books, they pushed the publication date back so many times that fans began threatening to picket their lobby). Between that extended delay, and the fact that the books were published more than a decade (or longer in some cases) after Sherri had written them, there is an accidental time warp in the first five books as the different copy editors working on them didn't realize that they were part of a series or that they weren't taking place during the year they were finally published. While trying to "fix" the timeline, the editors inadvertently created a continuity/time warp in the series that wasn't supposed to be there.

Sherri had her hands full updating the constantly changing technology and pop culture in the early books as the years went by, as well as some of the bands and slang. You can still see one bit of history that Sherri intentionally left in as a time capsule with Grace wearing a Duran Duran t-shirt. There are other Easter eggs in those early books if you pay attention that remain from their 1980s drafts.

In **Kiss of the Night**, *Wulf originally made references to* **Dark Shadows** *and* **The Lost Boys** *instead of* **Buffy the Vampire Slayer.** *Sherri didn't actually start watching the* **Buffy** *TV show until she was asked to participate in an anthology for it after* **Kiss of the Night** *was published.*

Astrid & Arina

Though this piece depicts Astrid and Zarek from the Dark-Hunters, Astrid was originally born during Sherri's years of moderating the role-playing game *Villains & Vigilantes* (daughter of Themis/Justice, get it?). At that time, Sherri dated one of the original writers for a group the world would very shortly come to know as White Wolf, and a vampire series known as *The Masquerade*.

Astrid was friends with another one of Sherrilyn's characters, Arina, a vigilante that Sherri role-played in college who became the heroine for her *Hellchaser* novel, *Daemon's Angel*, that was published in 1995. The original draft for *Daemon's Angel* was written while Sherri was an art major in college. Sherri still has her art portfolio where she drew the concept art for Arina while writing the story as a class project. She received an A for both.

In college, Sherri wanted to be a Creative Writing major. She applied three times to the program and was turned down each time. On her third application, the professor in charge of the program told her not to waste her time with another application as the program was reserved only for students who had a future as published authors (keep in mind that Sherri was published at the time she applied). She tried to switch her major to journalism but couldn't pass the typing test because her right hand is partially paralyzed (this was before schools had to make accommodations). And it should be noted that Sherri was not only an editor for her school paper, she'd had one of her stories picked up by the AP Wire when she was only eighteen. To this day, that story has made her a legend at Georgia College & State University where Sherri entered a side of beef into the Miss Georgia College Pageant to protest the new and unfair rules of cohabitation that had been made after Vanessa Williams had lost her crown. Sherri entered it and then wrote the story that became world famous in 1985. Yet the journalism school refused to accept her because of a birth defect that she has never allowed to slow her down or stop her, and one most people don't even notice.

Series Logo & Trademark

Why the bow & arrow? Aside from the fact that Artemis is the goddess of the hunt, Sherri has been an archer all her life and loves archery. She's also Sagittarius, Sagittarius rising. So, when she sat down to design an iconic symbol for her series, there was no other emblem she could envision for it.

When she first asked for the emblem and her series name to be placed on the books as a trademark, her publisher balked. At the time she made her request, it was unheard of for an author to trademark a series. While authors had series, no one had an identifier on the book, unless it was in the title itself, nor did authors have their own logos or trademarks. Sherrilyn changed all that.

Sherri's trademark of using a double bow goes back to college when she'd put one on her artwork or in her signature as a trademark like Nike did with the swoosh on their shoes.

OFFICIAL ® DARK-HUNTERS EMBLEM

UNDER THE PROTECTION OF

DARK-HUNTERS

Dark-Hunter.com

SYMBOL OF STRYKER'S SPATHI

Logos & Patches

The daughter of a career army sergeant and niece of a navy seaman, Sherri was fascinated by military patches and began collecting them as a girl. When she began writing her military League series in elementary school, she immediately started hand-drawing their badges and patches, for each rank, branch, and group, etc. So, it was only natural for her to create various logos and symbols for her Dark-Hunters when she started writing them in college. As the old saying goes, you write what you know and Sherri, being an art major in college and Army brat, also drew what she knew.

ST. RICHARD'S

NICKCHRONICLES.COM

DEADMAN'S CROSS
DEADMANSCROSS.COM

St. Michael's
Key

OFFICIAL
KENYON
MENYON

SK
MYKENYON
READ IT. LOVE IT.
SHERRILYNKENYON.COM

Sentella Troop Sleeve
Patches During
The Sentella-League War

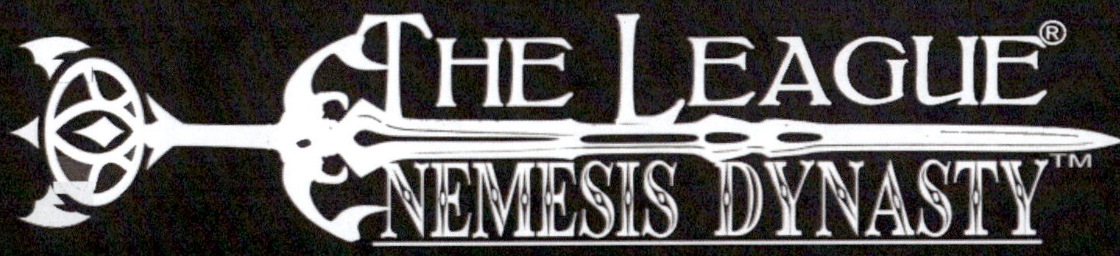

LEAGUE LOGOS
OVER THE YEARS

SANCTUM
SENTELLA
NEMESISRISING.COM

In Morte Veritas
LivetheLeague.com

IRIS
I REQUIRE INTENSE SUPERVISION

SAMARI

League Guilds & Logos

In Morte Veritas
LiveTheLeague.com

Command Assassin
Third Order
Badges and Emblems

LIVETHELEAGUE.COM

The League Ranks
Andarion LT Commander
Badges and Emblems

The League Ranks
Command Assassin
First Order
Badges and Emblems

™©Sherrilyn Kenyon
LiveTheLeague.com

KNIGHTS OF THE GRAIL
LORDS OF AVALON
DARK-HUNTER:® LORDS OF AVALON®

SPW
READ IT. LOVE IT.

AUTOGRAPHS

Sherri,

To a kind person whom I have shared three school years together, I wish the best in life. I hope that all your goals will be achieved (especially writing). I know that you have talent in that area and hope that you'll be successful.

Love ya, Judy

Sherri
To the most talented aspiring writer I have yet to meet. We had an interesting time in journalism this year. Keep up writing & have a great summer

John Jardin

Flight D

Class of "84"

To a very sweet young lady. I want you to stay that way because with your writing talent it'll take you far. I hope to have you in many classes next year. Love, Rigo Clement

"The Clem"

1980

Sherri,
You have so much talent and potential. I'll be watching to see how you use it to your best advantage.

J Marchman

1982

DARK HUNTERS®

Defying All Odds

Sherri first began selling and publishing the Dark-Hunter short stories in 1984. They appeared in a large number of small press magazines and journals between 1984-1989. Many times, she was paid only in copies of the magazines and not in actual money as that was a practice back in the eighties, since many small press magazines couldn't afford to pay writers for their work, and most writers were willing to work just for a copyright and byline.

While publishing the short stories and building her audience, Sherri continued to write the novels, even though she didn't know if they'd ever sell. That was what enabled her to present Kim Cardascia with the outline for over fifty-four Dark-Hunter novels when she first signed Sherri in the nineties. Those were books that Sherri had created in the eighties while in college, along with the drafts for the first Dark-Hunters that St. Martin's Press published.

In 1996, after publishing six bestselling books that included the #1 bestselling books of the League series, Sherri received over 150 rejections for *Night Pleasures*, *Night Embrace* and *Night Play*, alone. And yes, you heard that correctly. Over 150 rejections for two books that later received the Borders award for being the bestselling books of the year for their chain, and those books came out in the fall of that year. Those rejections also included the infamous letter from one editor that is forever seared into Sherri's memory: *No one at this publishing house will ever be interested in developing this author. Do not submit her work to us again.*

After that rejection, her now ex-husband demanded she quit writing. Sherri refused. She eventually sold Dark-Hunters to St. Martin's Press, to an editor who had rejected the series twice before finally buying it. Her editor had so little faith in the series, that she quickly passed Sherri and her Dark-Hunters off to her assistant so that her assistant could practice being an editor. It took SMP so long to release the first book (they kept pushing the release dates back) that Sherri's frustrated fans threatened to storm the Flat Iron building to get a copy of the manuscript.

When the book finally came out, it cleared the warehouse in less than two weeks and was out of stock for months because the publisher couldn't keep up with fan demand that kept it backordered for the first year.

Those eager fans are what caused *Night Pleasures* to hit an overall sales ranking on Amazon of #6 more than 10 months before its release date. Something that baffled Sherri's publisher who kept asking Sherri's sales reps why the book was so popular.

.

Dragonswan

St. Martin's delayed the release date of the first novel for so long, that one of Sherri's Dark-Hunter short stories that she'd written in the eighties and sold to Berkley ended up coming out before the first novel, which then messed up the sequence of events in the Dark-Hunter timeline. Sherri had to pull that short story and swap it for another one she'd written.

When her publisher found out, they insisted that she remove all mention of Dark-Hunter from the Berkley short story. Because Sherri had promised her fans a related Dark-Hunter short story to tide them over as they'd been waiting for almost two years for the first peep of the Dark-Hunters, Sherri refused. So, she removed the term Were-Hunter from Dragonswan, but let it go forward to Berkley, which made St. Martin's unhappy, but thrilled the fans. It still messed with the timeline, but not as badly.

BROGAN

Hard Times

Between 1992-1994, Sherri sold six books that went on to be bestsellers. Those books included the first three books of the #1 *New York Times* bestselling League series that Sherri had written in the eighties, and one of the Hellchasers novels, *Daemon's Angel*, which is a series related to the Dark-Hunters. But because her ex-husband had interfered with her career and after the premature birth of her oldest son, Sherri found herself pregnant and homeless with an infant in Columbus, Mississippi and unable to sell another book for four and a half years. The most horrifying part about that was the fact that her then in-laws refused to help them get back on their feet, by saying "you made your bed, you can lie in it." As if Sherri had planned for the catastrophic medical bills that had financially crippled their young family. Or the fact that the in-laws had refused to help pay for their son's law school debt—it was the stress of working three jobs to pay bills so that her husband could study while her own father was dying of cancer that had caused Sherri to deliver prematurely. Rather than help alleviate the stress on Sherri who was under bedrest for her tenuous health while pregnant, her in-laws only compounded it by heaping such cruelty on them as to repo Lawrence Kenyon's truck from them, leaving Sherri and her then-husband with only one aging car between them while her in-laws had four cars (two Corvettes, a Lincoln Town Car, and a Ram truck) for two people who had taken in a former maid's daughter and was paying for her to attend private school in Georgia and for her to visit her parents who lived in Hawaii several times a year.

Sherri's former in-laws were so selfish during this time, they would routinely take Sherri to seafood restaurants, knowing that she doesn't eat seafood and that she and her ex-husband couldn't afford to eat out, then refuse to even pay for their own grandsons (keeping in mind that they were again paying for the former maid's daughter to live with them full-time), leaving Sherri to starve so that she could buy her children and now ex-husband food while she ate the free bread and drank water. Sherri's mother couldn't afford to help them as Sherri's mother was also battling cancer, and the bulk of her mother's money went to pay for Sherri's older sister who has Cerebral Palsy, and whose medical bills had always taken the lion's share of her mother's income. That being said, no matter how poor Sherri's mother was, she never once ever allowed any of her children to pay for a single meal in her presence. The one thing Sherri's mother taught her daughter, parents provide for their children. It was a pity Sherri's in-laws never learned that lesson.

Birth of Kinley MacGregor

After four-and-half years of trying to publish again, and fighting with her ex-husband over her writing, and that one rejection that took the wind out of her sails, Sherri was ready to give up on her lifelong dreams. She's told the story a thousand times of how she was carrying me (Madaug) to the mailbox when she got the magazine that had an ad from her former agent who had become an editor at a publishing house. Though I don't remember it, I'm really glad I was there. Her mother had paid for her dues for the magazine as a Christmas present to keep her ex from yelling at her about the cost and when she saw her old agent's name, her heartbeat picked up. She wanted to submit, but was afraid to try, especially since her agent had been at another publisher where she'd kept the Dark-Hunters for two years and had tried to buy them but had been unable to get the concept past the marketing team at Dell. Too many years of being rejected haunted her.

Plus, Sherri didn't want another fight about her writing. Last thing she wanted was to take any more money away from her kids. So, she set the magazine aside and tried not to think about it. But Sherri is fearless and couldn't let it go. Her Dark-Hunters were calling, and so was her destiny. She went back and wrote what she claims is the worst query letter in history. She says that she actually put in it, "you probably don't remember me," and she was one of the agent's first clients.

That day, she stole a single stamp from her ex's wallet (because if she took two, he'd know that she'd sent in a proposal and there would have been a fight over it) and submitted to Laura Cifelli the proposal for the first Dark-Hunters and the first Deadman's Cross novel. Because no one was publishing paranormal, Sherri didn't mention that her pirate book had some of that in it. Laura called and told her that paranormal market was dead so she wasn't interested in the Dark-Hunters. But she wanted to see the pirate book that everyone had also told Sherrilyn would never sell. That included her most recent agent who had just parted ways with her over that very book, and her critique partners who were all *New York Times* bestselling authors who'd all told her that it was an impossible time period because no publishing house would ever touch that time period or subject.

Against the odds, Laura offered her a three book deal. But because these were to be straight historicals, she wanted them written under a new name.

Harper & Avon

Under Laura's brilliant guidance, Kinley took off like a rocket. According to Laura, the first book of the *Sea Wolves* (renamed from *Deadman's Cross* because Sherri fully intended to write the paranormal series someday and didn't want to lose the paranormal characters) had the highest print run for any first-time author in Harper Collins history at that time. It also made the Doubleday Book Club, which back then was an almost impossible feat for a genre book, and especially one for a "first-time" author. Laura put Sherri on a six month release schedule, and they were going like gangbusters.

Derailed Again

Sherri got a call out of the blue from Laura telling her to get an agent. Since Sherri had bad experiences with them—one of her past agents had been jailed for embezzlement, another had died and left her in a bad state, etc., Sherri wasn't really thrilled at the thought. But Laura was insistent and something in her tone told Sherri to listen. Because she didn't know whom to trust or where to go, Sherri asked Laura for a recommendation and Laura made the call for her.

A few days later, Sherri learned why. Laura had been fired out of the blue, and Sherri was abandoned. Her second book was moved from its six month slot to a year later, and she was told not only by the publisher, but other authors at Avon not to get comfy there as they had no intention of keeping any of the Harper authors even though Harper was the company that had bought out Avon. The Avon authors wouldn't even let Sherri join their community author loop (for a time Sherri jokingly called herself Rudolph the Red-Nosed Writer) that's how certain they were that she would be gone from their roster. So, Sherri began pressing her agent to submit her Dark-Hunters. Her agent was extremely reluctant because she didn't represent paranormal and no one was buying it.

When Avon finally reassigned Sherri a new editor, Monique Patterson called up and wanted Sherri to undo every single edit Laura had asked Sherri to do in the book she'd rewritten for Laura.

But Sherri didn't want to destroy the book, so she told Monique that she had another idea she'd had from college that Laura had passed on and because she'd had the idea and characters for so long, she could write it fast.

However, since Sherri had just given birth to Ian and we had moved from Jackson, MS to a very rural Spring Hill, TN, where we didn't have any cable, or telephone or even a grocery store or cellphone towers at the time, Monique didn't believe she could do it. But impossible tasks are Sherrilyn's specialty. So at home alone with two toddlers and an infant and no delivery whatsoever or modern convenience, Sherri wrote Draven's book in less than a month.

Avon was so impressed, and her sales numbers were so strong, they moved her to a lead title slot. Eventually, the other authors had to admit that Sherrilyn was there to stay.

Return to Sherrilyn Kenyon

Even though Sherrilyn believed in them, no one would take a chance on the Dark-Hunters. Sherrilyn kept nagging her Avon editor, Monique to try the series that her fans were clamoring for. Monique liked them but couldn't get them past the higher ups at Avon.

Finally, St. Martin's, after losing a major auction for another author to Avon decided to make a low-ball offer for Sherri's Dark-Hunters. Even though it was a major cut in pay that her then-husband was furious at her for taking because her regular pay wasn't all that high to begin with, Sherri jumped at it.

Avon was also furious at Sherrilyn for daring to write paranormals. It didn't matter that they had told her not to get comfy in their house or that they had turned down the Dark-Hunters repeatedly, they were so convinced the market was dead that they refused to let Sherri use the Kinley MacGregor name she'd created and built on them. They didn't want her to jeopardize "their" books or sales with what they were convinced was a failure waiting to happen.

Disappointed they couldn't use the Kinley MacGregor name Sherrilyn had been building, St. Martin's told Sherri to go back to using her real name as they figured she might have "some" readers out there who might remember some of her books from the early nineties. And yes, it was stated that way to her. This is where I should remind everyone that Sherri sold out her first signing in the nineties in less than forty-five minutes while sitting next to a bestselling author who was so upset by it and the steady stream of fans that she kept rudely grabbing Sherrilyn's books from the table and asking, "Who are you? Are you somebody famous? Should I know who you are?" And that Sherri had the largest first print run for Kinley MacGregor in Harper history.

For whatever reason, publishers have always underestimated Sherrilyn's readership and fanbase.

So, Kinley MacGregor returned to Sherrilyn Kenyon at St. Martin's. And even though Sherrilyn Kenyon hit a number of bestseller lists first, it was Kinley who simultaneously landed the first two books on the *New York Times* list, and Sherrilyn Kenyon who hit #1 on the *New York Times*. Something that enraged Avon even though they were the house that had refused to even look at the Dark-Hunters. Their anger was such that their publisher not only publicly shamed and embarrassed Sherri at a dinner party before the other authors and publishing professionals in attendance, she made Sherri sit at the kiddie table in a dark corner because of it (normally bestselling authors sit in the front at the publisher's table and not only was Sherri the best bestseller they had in that room, she was the only #1 bestselling author in attendance when the publisher shamed her in front of her peers and colleagues).

APOLLYMI
DARK-HUNTER

ダーク ハンター
DARK HUNTER
PWN
THE
DARKNES
NOFEAR
FIREWALL
BLACK

Dark-Hunters Manga

Dark-Hunters was chosen to be an OEL (original English language) manga. Sherri wanted to pitch it to a manga press, but SMP refused to let it go. They bought the first two novels and adapted *Night Pleasures* and *Night Embrace*. *Night Pleasures* instantly hit the *New York Times* bestseller list, unseating the male dominated chart, and not only making Sherri the only female on the manga list, but the only American. In spite of that, and in spite of fan enthusiasm, SMP refused to continue on with more books as it was not what they normally publish. And since the Dabel Bros. sold their company to Marvel, Sherri and her fans were again left adrift and the rights were tied up . . .

Marvel

After Sherrilyn moves to a new agent, she finally realizes her lifelong dream of being published by Marvel, even though Marvel, DC, IDW and Dark Horse all turned down the Dark-Hunters back in the eighties when she submitted them to the comics publishers. However, it isn't the official Dark-Hunters that Marvel publishes, but rather their spin-off series, the Lords of Avalon.

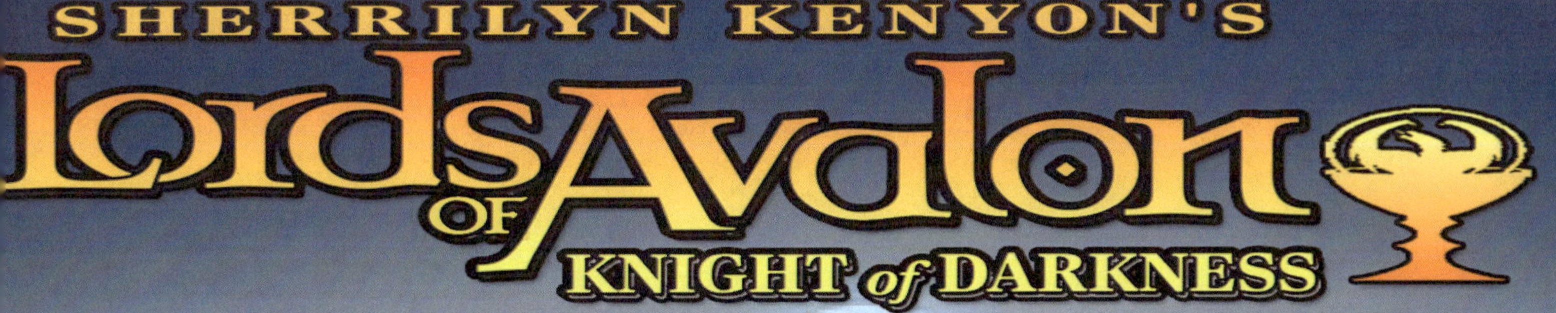

SHERRILYN KENYON'S
Lords Avalon
OF
KNIGHT of DARKNESS
FROM THE WORLD OF DARK HUNTERS

Lords of Avalon

Sherrilyn came up with the idea for the Lords of Avalon while in college, during her Celtic Twilight class. While working on a paper about the Arthurian Legends, her mind began whirling with the question of what happened the day after the battle of Camlann? What did Morgen do?

What happened to the knights of the Round Table?

She began working on the stories that afternoon.

Originally, the LOA were part of the Dark-Hunters. But when Avon became angry over the fact that Sherrilyn's Dark-Hunter fame was bypassing and overshadowing her Kinley MacGregor name, they wanted a piece of that pie. In order to placate them, she carved out that tiny sliver of the Dark-Hunter universe. That is why the first two LOA novels, *Sword of Darkness* and *Knight of Darkness* are published under the Kinley MacGregor name, and the rest were moved to St. Martin's to be published as Sherrilyn Kenyon (there's also more to this story, but that's for my mom to tell at a later date).

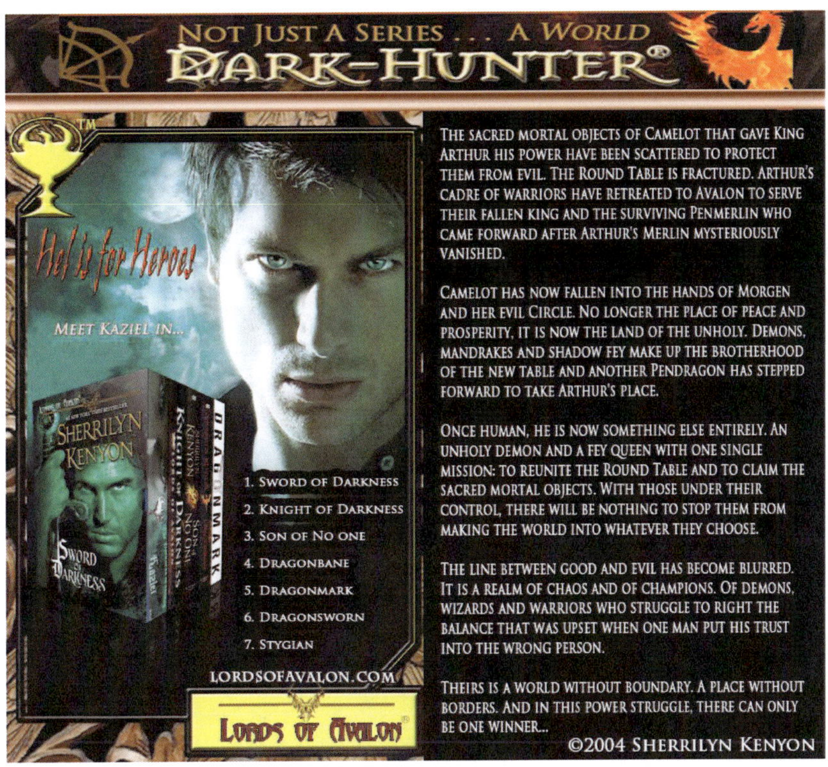

A Whole New World

The sacred mortal objects of Camelot that gave King Arthur his power have been scattered to protect them from evil. The Round Table is fractured. Arthur's cadre of warriors have retreated to Avalon to serve their fallen king and the surviving Penmerlin who came forward after Arthur's Merlin mysteriously vanished.

Camelot has now fallen into the hands of Morgen and her evil Circle. No longer the place of peace and prosperity, it is now the land of the unholy. Demons, mandrakes and shadow fey make up the brotherhood of the new table and another Pendragon has stepped forward to take Arthur's place.

Once human, he is now something else entirely. An unholy demon and a fey queen with one single mission: to reunite the Round Table and to claim the sacred mortal objects. With those under their control, there will be nothing to stop them from making the world into whatever they choose.

The line between good and evil has become blurred.

It is a realm of chaos and of champions. Of demons, wizards and warriors who struggle to right the balance that was upset when one man put his trust into the wrong person.

Theirs is a world without boundary. A place without borders. And in this power struggle, there can only be one winner . . .

SHERRILYN KENYON'S
Lords of Avalon
SWORD of DARKNESS

Morgen Le Fey

As evil as she ever was, Morgen leveraged everything to kill her brother and claim his throne. What she never expected was to lose her son in the process. But that's okay. Maternal instinct never came easy to her, anyway. Now she rules over her evil Circle and plots a way to lay waste to Merlin so that she can break free, into the human realm and finish what she started.

While Mordred isn't dead, he sleeps with his life force tied to that of Arthur's eldest son. When one wakes, the other will awaken and finish the battle that fatally wounded them in medieval England.

Lord Darkness

As the merlin for Caliburn, Kerrigan rose up to replace Arthur as the king of Morgen's Camelot. Until the merlin of Excalibur steps forward, he is the most powerful of the merlins who answer to the one Penmerlin. However, in Kerrigan's case, he answers to Morgen. And everyone in her court answers to him.

Or his sword.

Sword of Darkness

In the first book of the series, everything changes for Kerrigan when Morgen assigns him the task of locating and capturing Seren, the merlin of Caswallen's Loom. As the great-great-great-great-granddaughter of Emrys Penmerlin, Seren is a rare gem for Morgen's crown. Morgen knows if she can get the two of them together, she will produce a baby who will unseat the current Merlin and be able to reign over a new Round Table and the Dark Camelot she's trying to build.

Second Chances

But as with many best laid plans, things don't go quite the way Morgen plans. Or Kerrigan for that matter. And in the end, the king of Camelot learns that some of the strongest magick in the universe isn't the kind you're born with or that can be commanded.

It's a whole different kind that you never see coming.

(issue 1 variant cover by Tom Grummett, Terry Pallot and Guru eFX)

Grail Symbol

The Lords of Avalon grail symbol was originally designed by Sherrilyn when she was in high school. The concept of a basic cup came from watching the old film, *Excalibur*. On her wall, she kept a framed piece of newsprint where she spent years working on a castle drawing. In the corner of that drawing is where she sketched her first draft of the iconic emblem for her series.

Sherri added the phoenix rising from the center of the grail during her sophomore year when she decided to add Arthur's son, Draig, to the mix. She wanted an emblem that would mix the original Arthurian legend and her more modern spin on the tale.

Knight of Darkness

For countless centuries, Varian du Fey has been the assassin for the infamous Merlin, even though the woman who birthed him sits at the right hand of his enemy, Morgen le Fey. Now both his mother and Morgen have decided that it's time Varian takes his place on their side of this conflict.

Normally, telling them no wouldn't be a problem, except for the fact that the good guys Varian protects believe him to be an even worse demon than the ones they fight.

Maybe they're right. After all, Varian does love a good maiming of anyone who gets in his way.

At least until his mother gives him a simple choice: join Morgen's Circle of the Damned or see an innocent woman die.

Varian's all for saving the innocent, but Merewyn isn't as innocent as she seems. And she's none too fond of the fact that her fate is in the dubious hands of the son of the evil Adoni who cursed her. Normally, Varian would have no problem leaving her to her own means, but leaving her to Morgen is rough, even for him.

Now the only way to save both their lives is to face the evilest forces ever known—his mother and Morgen. And two people who know nothing of trust must learn to rely on each other or die: provided they don't kill each other first.

PHILIP TAN '07
JEFF
DE LOS SANTOS

Minions of Death

Varian's book introduces readers to all kinds of new and fun creatures who inhabit Avalon and Camelot. Besides getting a closer look at the Adoni and their culture, readers get to see the Charontes meaner cousins—the minions of death or MODs. Scary demons, they'll devour anything.

Even each other.

Goylestones

While mandrakes and gargoyles peppered the pages of *Sword of Darkness*, their adorable little counterparts are introduced in *Knight of Darkness*. One of the most unforgettable characters is little Beau, the most lovable rock to ever roll into someone's life.

Beau, as well as Varian, also makes a reappearance in *Dragonsworn*.

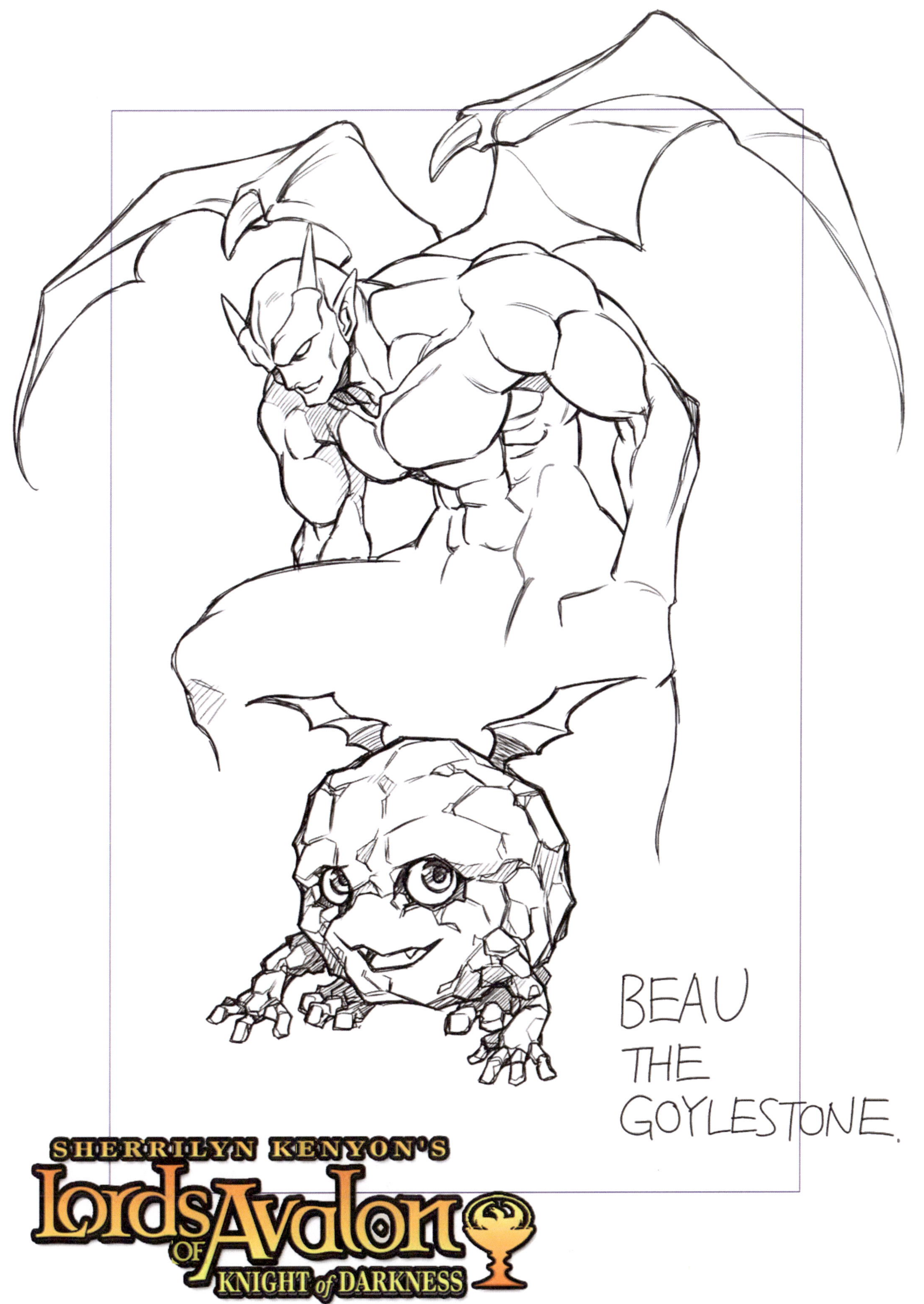

BEAU
THE
GOYLESTONE.

SHERRILYN KENYON'S
Lords of Avalon
KNIGHT of DARKNESS

The Future Is Ours

Who better to merge their evilness than Apollo and Morgen? Not only are they rivals, but now they're partners, ready to take over the world and claim it,

Let the best evil win . . .

Chronicles of Nick

I would say the idea for Sherrilyn to write Young Adult is as old as Sherrilyn, but my mom might get offended. So instead, I'll say that one of her oldest stories was written for a younger audience.

When she first thought about the Dark-Hunters, she immediately envisioned a younger group of Squires who would have their own set of stories to go along with the adult version of the books. Hence Nick's conception and why he was such a key player in the series. From the very beginning, Sherrilyn wanted to write his story, but getting it past her publisher wasn't easy.

Over and over, she was told that no one would read a series with a male protagonist. That teenage boys didn't read and that girls wouldn't be interested in reading a series that was focused on a boy in the lead.

Until the day I came home from middle school and told her that I was desperate for something to read that had a zombie in it. Mom . . . er, Sherrilyn, took up the challenge and went after her publisher with a vengeance.

Ironically, she'd already sold another YA series, Nevermore, but her publisher was putting it on the back burners, wanting her to focus more on the adult titles for a while longer. However, in 2005, Sherrilyn became determined and began nagging all her publishers again until she finally got a full committal on the project.

But even with the go-ahead, it would take a full five more years before they'd finally put them to press.

Chronicles of Nick immediately shot to #1 on all the major lists.

My Name Is Nick Gautier

The world of the Dark-Hunters® is unlike anything you've ever seen before. It's dark. It's gritty. It's dangerous . . . And it's a whole lot of fun and a lot of laughs.

My name is Nicholas Ambrosius Gautier, and this is the story of my life.

First off, get the name right. It's pronounced Go-shay not Go-tee-ay or Goat-chay (that has an extra H in it and as my mom says we're so poor we couldn't afford the extra letter). I'm not some fancy French fashion designer. I'm just a regular kid . . . well as regular as someone with a stripper for a mother and a career felon for a father can be.

But as my mom so often says friends are what God gives us to make up for the families we're born into. And my mother, in spite of her occupation, is a lady and I'll fight anyone who says otherwise. Consider this your notice. You respect Cherise Gautier or I'll learn you better.

My kingdom is the French Quarter and here I reign as prince. Everyone knows me and I know them.

Now I'm not doing bad for a kid whose education is from the backstreets and alleys. I sweep floors in the doll store along with a few other unmentionable jobs my mom would kill me over if she knew about. I even work as a guide on the "Undead of New Orleans" tours. Everyone who visits the Quarter either takes one or runs into one of these tours passing on the street. You know them. "And on this spot something spooky happened" or some other load of bull. Heck, I make most of it up each night just to keep from being bored.

I mean really, demons? Werewolves? Gods and goddesses on the streets (other than those being portrayed on the Mardi Gras floats)? Vampires? Who believes that crap?

The only blood-suckers I ever saw were the lawyers in their expensive suits and big butt mosquitoes (if you've ever been to New Orleans, then you know about the B-52 bombers I'm talking about). Besides, now that Anne Rice has moved out of town, she took the lot of that with her. We're a vamp-free zone.

And then one night, I decided that even though I'd done a lot of bad things in my life, I wasn't about to shake down a couple of tourists no matter how much money they had and I didn't. So instead of beating on some innocents, the guys I hung with beat on me.

They'd have killed me, too, had it not been for this mysterious dude who came out of nowhere and struck them down so fast that all I could see was a black blur. The next thing I know, I'm a part of a world I'd never imagined in my wildest dreams. And my dreams can be pretty rowdy.

The Dark-Hunters call them Daimons, but I call them scary as all get out. Soul-sucking demons, they're controlled by a ruthless goddess who has been trapped in a realm she despises. Now it's a game on between the goddess Apollymi and the Dark-Hunter Acheron.

The winner takes the world.

The Secret of Nick

According to Sherri, the Nick Chronicles *is* Nick's real and true past. It's both a prequel and sequel to the Dark-Hunters. And there's a huge surprise (several actually) in the series that I'm not allowed to spoil, but when you read them, everything you think is an inconsistency will make perfect sense to you. More than that, you will understand exactly why Nick is the way he is and what is happening the world of the Dark-Hunters.

Remember the one promise that Sherri always tries to keep in every book: Just when you think you know the truth about a character or event, you find out that things are seldom what they seem. Nick is one of those characters. There's a lot more to our little Cajun than what you've seen to date.

There are many, many secrets in this universe and by following Nick and crew, you'll learn all kinds of new information about a lot of characters, including Cherise and especially Jaden and Jared. Just hold on . . . you ain't seen nothing yet!

Nyria Belami Anaxkolasi

Better known as Nekoda Kennedy or Kody, she's one of the fresh faces introduced in the Nick Chronicles. The daughter of Styxx and Bethany, she becomes Nick's anchor and one of the major players in both the CON, and DH books. But we don't want to give too many secrets away, so that's all we can say about her at this time . . .

Bubba Burdette

Sherri often says that no character is based on anyone in her real life, but Big Bubba Burdette (Triple B) is the rare exception. He's based on her big brother Buddy (the original Triple B). Right down to his love of horror movies, zombies, computers, football, and flannel shirts. It's all an homage to the brother she lost.

And everyone loves Bubba's snarky humor and knack for getting into trouble. Not to mention his sidekick, Mark Fingerman who's named after another friend of Sherri's.

Kaziel

Nick's shapeshifting friend was originally slated to be part of the Lords of Avalon series and had his own book, *Darkness Within*, that should have come out in 2007 . . . but something happened that we're not at liberty to talk about at this time.

One day, however, my mother will be telling the whole story of what really happened with *Darkness Within* and why the Lords of Avalon were pulled aside for so long. It's quite an interesting tale, and one that it sure to leave you with a slack-jaw at the horrific things that go on in the publishing world behind closed doors. Especially to established, #1 bestselling authors and their series.

But Kaziel has enjoyed his resurgence in the CON novels, as has Vawn and Xev. We definitely haven't seen the last of them and they will be back in the near future!

Simi

Like many of the Dark-Hunter characters, Simi makes frequent appearances alongside Nick and his friends. For those who are fans of both series, you've even met her children . . . in the future. And you've already met her husband, you just don't know it yet.

DARK-HUNTER

I Thought CON Had 14 Books?

Intensity is the last "official" book of the Nick Chronicles. Due to the bad behavior of a certain group of former employees who shall remain nameless (but fans know who they are), the series ended up being cut in half because of their scandalous antics against our mother and her fans. As a result, the publisher kept moving the date of book eight back in their schedule.

Because our mother is a woman of her word, she promised her fans that she wouldn't have *Intensity* moved again. So, when St. Martin's decided to move it one more time due to the antics of said people above, Sherrilyn bought it back and published it herself to ensure the fans wouldn't have to wait on it. But that meant that the book had to be rewritten so that the series could be "split" and have a temporary ending that she hadn't meant for it to have.

As a result, the official Chronicles of Nick series is now only eight books long.

Into the Future

But don't despair! Sherrilyn intends to continue the series with *Shadows of Fire,* where we focus on the Cyprian Malachai, and Ambrose for four books.

After those four books are written, Sherrilyn will bring us back to the present where we will see the current "Nick" and have his adult novels for a separate four book series, Shadowland Riders. This way no one will mistake the last four of the series as YA.

SHADOWS OF FIRE™

Nevermore

For those who don't know, the Nick Chronicles, aren't the only YA that Sherrilyn has written and published. Long before she created the Dark-Hunters, Sherri conceived and drafted the post-apocalyptic world of Nevermore with Josiah Crow and crew, Back when she was just a girl in elementary school, Sherri was entranced with H.G. Wells and Edgar Allen Poe. It was while watching *War of the Worlds* with her older brother on a late night movie marathon that she had the brainstorm for has now become its bestselling short story that Sherri first wrote when she was in fourth grade.

St. Martin's originally had the series under contract back in the early 2000s before they contracted for the Nick Chronicles and had intended to release it back in 2006 when they bought CON. Longtime fans well remember the Nevermore site that was up back in 2003-2008. But sadly St. Martin's back-burnered the series and never released it.

In 2016, due to the actions of Sherrilyn's ex-husband, St. Martin's cancelled the contract and returned the rights of the series to her. Sherri released the original short story, Insurrection, to her fans, and it was an overnight sensation. Hopefully, the trilogy she drafted so long ago and that fans have been begging to read for almost twenty years will soon be out! They and Sherri have certainly been waiting long enough!

Josiah's Promise

This old world ain't what it used to be. Humanity was just minding its own business when all of a sudden, spaceships filled the skies. It was First Contact. See the Drabs had been searching for a planet that was rich in Specularite (gray hematite for those unfamiliar with the term). It's a mineral they use for medicine and fuel. They'd come here to set up negotiations with us.

But there's an old earth saying, the road to hell is paved with good intentions. They brought with them Hyrotitus. A germ that was as common to them as the sniffles. To humans, it was lethal. Those who were young and those who were old perished within days of contracting it. The only to survive were adolescents whose bodies were changing, and a handful of exceptionally strong adults. Somehow the germ mutated them, making them stronger, smarter . . . more lethal. It left us with incredible abilities that the Drabs didn't count on. In the old days, our ancestors would have called us "magical."

The Drabs could have saved us. They had the medicine and technology. Some of them wanted to and they had a small and brief civil war over it. In the end, it was decided that we weren't worth saving. That they wanted our planet and we were nothing more than a nuisance to them. Not worth their time or their resources.

Human survivors were forced underground as the Drabs began destroying everything that had been our proudest accomplishments—our literature, our art and cultures. For a hundred years mankind has tried to assimilate or hide. We identify each other by quoting human text. If we say, "To be or not to be," and the person looks at us as if we're insane, we know they're a Drab. But if they counter with another quote such as "Quoth the raven, nevermore" then we know they're one of us.

Now we're through with that. Hiding is for the old and infirmed. We are the Scraps of humanity, and we're pissed. This is our planet, our world, and we're taking it back. Drabs take note and take cover.

It's time to bring out *your* body bags.

SHERRILYN KENYON

NEVERMORE
BOOK 1

INSURRECTION

EVERY CROW HAS ITS MURDER

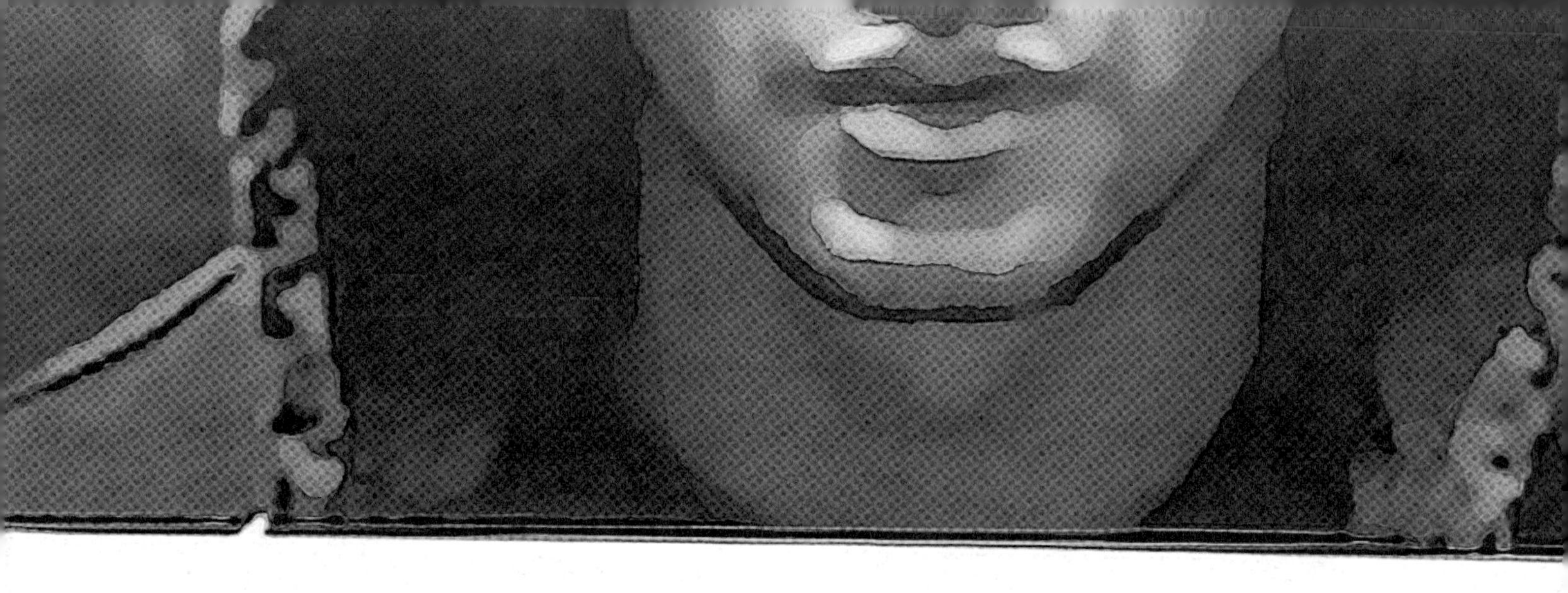
#REVOLUTION

Intercepted Broadcast 2190

The virus ran swiftly on the hot summer breeze. Unseen. Unheard. Unknown. It swept through the entire earth in a matter of months, having mercy on no one. Young–old–it didn't matter.

Brought to us by the Drabs, it was the last thing we expected. But the Drabs knew. They even fought a war over whether or not they should save us.

In the end, it was decided that we were diseased insects who were unfit to breathe their air.

Our air.

So, they left the human race to die a miserable death of agonizing pain. Left us with no doctors or medicine. Their plan was to rid the earth of us and to take our home as their own.

What they never expected was the change that would come after the plague. We didn't all die as they'd planned. Those under the age of twenty somehow managed to survive the disease.

We managed to pull through it, even alone, and we learned to hide ourselves while our bodies changed. Still human, but now something else. Something more powerful. More intuitive.

More pissed off.

We're still here, on this earth, and we're not leaving. This is our home.

Our planet.

Drabs take note and learn to be afraid. You've had a hundred years here on earth, but now your time here is done.

You called us rodents. Insects. Diseased animals. The scraps of humanity–and that, my Drab friend, we certainly are. But what you should have realized is that you can't kill a Scrap. Humanity isn't dead. Not by a long shot. We still have our soldiers and we have our conviction.

Most of all, we have hope.

And we will win in the end. Whatever it takes. Whatever it costs. We won't allow you to take our planet from us. So count your days, Drabs.

The war is on.

Hellchasers/Hell-Hunters

Long before time began, a war was fought between the powers of light and darkness. From their blood sprang some of the deadliest preternatural predators ever conceived. Demons and others so evil, no one could fight them. Mankind was left to cower and fall victim to their cruelty.

Until a pact was made . . .

We are the silent soldiers sent in to combat the worst of all evils- demons so terrifying even the bravest exorcist runs. When something breaks free from its hell, we are the ones sent in to retrieve it, banish it or kill it. Led by the mysterious Thorn, we are shapeshifters, demons and other souls who were damned by either knowing too much or treading down the path best left undisturbed . . . Sometimes we started out even worse than the ones we're sent after.

The only thing that unites us is our commitment to stand strong and to battle to the bitter end. Pray you never become one of our targets.

Most of all, pray we never fall.

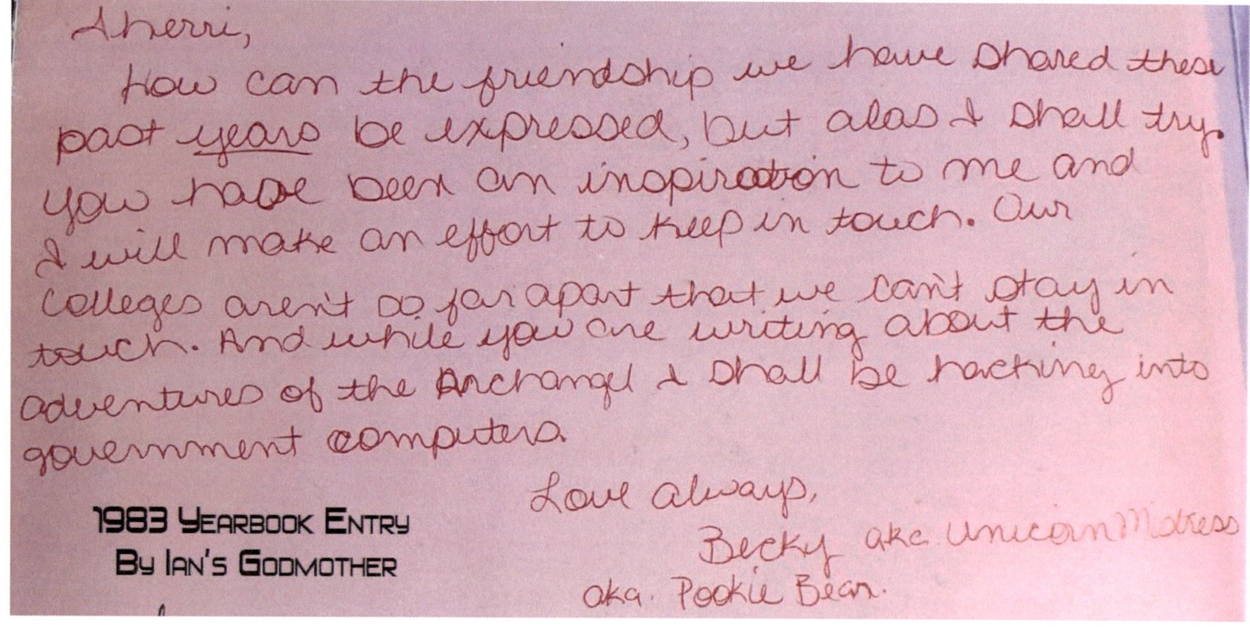

**1983 YEARBOOK ENTRY
BY IAN'S GODMOTHER**

Among the Dark-Hunter spin-offs is the well-known group lead by Thorn. Originally started by Sherrilyn in high school as a set of short stories about a group of humans chosen by archangels to send demons back to hell, the stories evolved over her college years into the group we know today and were in fact, the precursors to the Dark-Hunters. Sherri merged them with the Hunter Legends/Dark-Hunter universe in the mid 1980s.

#1 NEW YORK TIMES BEST-SELLING AUTHOR
SHERRILYN KENYON'S
DARK HUNTERS
HELLCHASER
DABEL BROTHERS
SAN DIEGO COMIC-CON EXCLUSIVE

ZEKE IN SERAPH FORM

Zeke Jacobson

You can tell just how old the Hell-Hunters are by the fact that Zeke is one of the very few characters that is named after someone Sherrilyn knows. She very rarely does that. His last name pays homage to Sheri Jacobs who grew up around the corner from Sherrilyn and still lives around the corner from Sherrilyn's brother, our uncle Steven. Fans who've been around have seen Sheri at many events over the years. They first met when mom was in fifth grade.

The concept for the Hellchasers comes from Sherrilyn's own grandfather who was a faith-healer and a Baptist preacher. Her mother was born in a revival tent, according to family legend, during one of his sermons. And Sherri grew up, listening to his stories about the demons in the bible needing to be driven back to nether regions where they belong.

Thorn

The concept of Thorn was simple. If everyone deserved a second chance, then surely even the most evil should be able to redeem themselves.

The Lily Among the Thorns. As a son of the purest evil, who better to understand it and fight against it? It goes with our mother's belief that no one should be judged by their circumstances or damned for the things they can't help, Her core belief that everyone can rise above the worst slings and arrows that life hurls and them. If they believe and fight hard enough, that any and everyone can defy their fate and what other people claim to be their "destiny" to make their own future, in spite of what others say. We've seen it ourselves. She won't let anyone define her. Nor will she bend her morality or compromise her faith for any reason. In the middle of a hurricane, she stands strong against it.

Deadman's Cross

From the magical realms of Dark-Hunters and Hellchasers, Sherrilyn returns to the Golden Age of Piracy that she wrote back in the 1980s to pen a trilogy of books unlike any other. Join Thorn and other Hunter/Hellchaser favorites as they hold the line against the latest evil the Mavromino has unleashed against humanity.

Hell On Earth . . .

When the Chthonians brought the primal gods to a truce at the end of their great war, part of the pact they forged was that the worst of the evil the gods had unleashed against each other and mankind would be forever banished.

But forever is a long time. And nothing can contain those determined to find a way back.

To catch evil, it takes evil . . .

While Thorn is able to contain the demons unleashed on the ground, the ones who prey on the innocent sailors and seafaring travelers are beyond his reach.

For the sake of humanity, he makes a shaky alliance with an old foe, Devyl Bane and his enchanted ship, Marcelina. Bane is one of the most notorious and bloodthirsty pirates to ever sail the high seas and one of the deadliest warlords ever born.

Damned and murdered by his own, Bane is out for revenge. With his own secret agenda, he agrees to take charge of the motley crew of pirates and brigands, and to protect the seas from the preternatural terrors that seek to devour every unwary soul they can take.

Theirs is a sacred and deadly task, as they are hunted by their prey and human authorities alike. If they fail, the world will fall to the ancient gods of chaos– Bane's one time allies and now enemies– and anarchy will reign. Most of all, the Southern gate, where the greatest, most powerful darkness is imprisoned, will be opened and there will be no stopping it.

It's yo ho ho and a bottle of high seas stakes where the souls of all humanity are the ultimate prize and bargaining chip. Here is where the Deadmen tell their tales.

Blackheart Bart

Devyl Bane's first mate and quartermaster, Bartholomew James Meers (Blackheart Bart) is another character who takes his name from a real person. He's named for one of Sherri's great-great-grandfathers who was an actual seafarer around the time the Deadman's Cross trilogy is set. Just as James Barnet is another relative of Sherri's (and a real historical pirate hunter and pirate who captured Calico Jack and Anne Bonney).

Since Sherri grew up boating, with her father telling her tales of the sea and of old family legends and stories, she wanted to incorporate her family's history in some of her books.

Sadly in real life, Bart wasn't a Simeon Magi. He came across Blackbeard in one of his voyages from England to America, and perished in the battle against the infamous pirate during their confrontation.

Jalen Wall, who works for Sherri, is a direct descendent of Blackbeard. It's a strange coincidence that the two of them adore each other given what happened between their great-great-great-grandfathers.

Belle Morte

Belle is another character taken from Sherri's early short stories that she wrote while in middle and high school. Back then she was one of the Hell-Hunters like Zeke. A necrodemian who took nothing from no one. But once Sherri split the necrodemians in half and created their Hellchaser cousins, Belle was moved into Thorn's group. She was, after all, too spunky to just follow along.

Valynda Moore

Sherrilyn first began collecting voodoo dolls when she was a little girl and her godmother gave her one. Fascinated by the wide variety and diversity of their styles, she's always kept them near and has amassed an amazing collection over the years.

The idea of turning one into a living creature was something she started playing around with when she was a little kid. Mostly due to her mother's active imagination where she would tell Sherri that the dolls she'd collected would come alive and follow her around the house. To make it seem real, her mother would move them around and put them in unlikely places such as closets, planters, drawers, etc., where Sherri would never expect to find them.

So it was only natural for Sherri to turn one of her favorite memories into a character for her short stories and then later, her books.

Marcelina of the Deruvians

Two of the first pantheons Sherri studied was Celtic and Norse, which then led her into studying the druids. Because of their deep roots (pardon the pun) with tree lore, it got her thinking of a unique race of tree people. It also didn't help that her grandparents had thirty acres of woods where she grew up. Thirty acres with some weirdly shaped trees that got her imagination going . . .

There was also a legend that the woods were haunted.

At any rate, Sherri would go and wander the woods, hiking for hours, sitting down to pen notes and think of characters such as Mara and others who she later used to populate her numerous series.

Dogs of War

While the Deadman's Cross trilogy is set in the past of the Dark-Hunters, there's a lot more to look forward to in the future.

Remember that Sherrilyn began writing the Hellchasers in middle school and the Dark-Hunters in 1984. And like we said, when she met Rickey Mallory in the early nighties, she already had well over a hundred published Dark-Hunter short stories, dozens of novels and the ideas for a lot more. That was why when she finally sold the series to St. Martin's, she gave her editor a list of fifty-four novels, and out of that list, she's only done two.

The Dogs of War were part of that list. Conceived in college as part of one of her role-playing groups, they are the baddest of the Dark-Hunters. Those so haunted by their past, that they bend to no one's rules and couldn't care less about pain. They will not be controlled.

Not even by Acheron.

This is why Ash called them in to help guard and corral the Malachai. After all, they are suicidal,

Though the DoWs were a large of the old short stories, and the original web site, the first published novel to feature one of their breed is Samia's story, *No Mercy* in 2010. The second one is *Queen of All Shadows* with Xander, one of the original books Sherri drafted while in college.

MAD. BAD. AND IMMORTAL.
DOGS OF WAR
BASED ON THE #1 BESTSELLING DARK-HUNTER NOVELS BY
SHERRILYN KENYON
ARISTIA

Yum!
Barbecue

Will There Be More Simi?

Of course! Simi will return in all her glory!

But Will She Have Her Own Book?

Technically, she already has her own book. *Simi's ABCs.* But we know that isn't what you mean. For those who've been reading and keeping up with the Nick Chronicles. Then you've met some of her kids, and you know that she will eventually marry.

As for when that story's told . . . that depends on a lot of variables. Yet with luck, we will one day have the story fans have been begging for.

Will Artemis Have Her Own Book?

If she doesn't die. At least that's what Sherrilyn always says. But if it makes you feel better, she loves all her characters equally. Even the villains. They are her children, after all, which means that she does have a book planned for her, as she does for every character. But sadly, the characters sometimes have other plans and they don't always agree with what she wants them to do. So, while she makes plans for them, they sometimes do the last thing she wants for them . . . such as die valiantly.

We don't think Artemis will, but Sherri always puts in a disclaimer, just in case.

Will Styxx Return?

Of course! He's been in several books since his, and he'll be in future books. And since his daughter is a major part of the Nick Chronicles, you know he'll be around for those as well.

But will he have another book with Bethany?

Sherri never says never. At the moment, there's not one planned, but in the future . . .
We'll see.

Will Katra Return?

Basically the same answer as Styxx. Given that she's Acheron's daughter, you know she'll be back. Most likely with kids. So stay tuned!

What About Acheron?

As the Dark-Hunter leader, you know he'll be around. And not just in the Dark-Hunters, but he's also a key play in the Nick Chronicles and a part of the Deadman's Cross and other series. So never despair, Acheron will return and so with Tory and the kids.

What About . . ?

Sherri's stock answer is always: if they don't die. As we said before, she loves all the characters equally, even the villains. She has many, many plans and ideas for the future. So, please be patient. We can't wait to see what's coming either! In the meantime, you can always check out her site: QueenofAllShadows.com for all the latest info on what's coming next. And of course, stop by Facebook.com/mysherrilyn to visit with us and the rest of her Paladins to chat with her and her fans. We are, after all, one big, happy family!

Before There Was Dark-Hunters

Most people mistakenly believe that Sherrilyn's career began in 2002, with the publication of the first Dark-Hunters novel. But as we've seen, her career started a long time before that.

Though she started writing novels in the 1970s and 1980s, she didn't sell her first book until 1991. The first three series she published were 1) The League: Nemesis Rising. 2) The League: Nemesis Legacy. 3) Hellchasers. In that order.

Those who've read the original white-cover edition of Born of the Night have actually read the version of the book that Sherri wrote when she was eighteen to twenty years old.

The League

In the Ichidian Universe, no one was safe. People were routinely dragged from their homes and killed in the streets-victims of a ruthless tyrant hellbent on being the sole ruler of every known government. Those who opposed his ruthless dictates and brutal taxes formed an alliance called The League of the Beleaguered.

After they put down Justicale Cruel and his supporters, the League realized that the best way to keep trouble from returning was to quickly and quietly cut it off at its head, whenever and wherever it sprouted. And toward that objective, they knew a separate group of elite soldiers was needed, and thus The League Assassins were born. Highly trained and highly valued, they became the backbone of the current watch-guard for the Nine Worlds.

But not even the League is immune to corruption . . .

Welcome to a world where corrupt assassination politics dominate everything and everyone. Where any moment no matter how circumspect you are, you can find yourself at the end of an assassin's blade or rifle, if the price is right. It's kill or be killed. You're either the hunter or the prey, and every life has a price.

Most live in fear. We fight back. These are the men and women who come from the streets and from bloodied backgrounds of survival. You just have to decide if they're better than the ones chasing you . . .

Or worse.

Sarcastic, loyal, highly trained and lethal, these men and women are the next generation of heroes who have banded together to protect the innocent from the corrupt governments and The League that prey on those who can't stand against them. They know how to laugh in the face of madness and danger, and to endure the worst The League and her enemies can hurl at them. They will not stand by and watch greed, tyranny and injustice tear their worlds apart.

The war is on . . .

United Systems Flag

The League

"Kenyon boldly goes where no author has gone before and claims yet another genre as her own. With her League series, she has created a new, addictive universe and proven herself the undisputed master of the cross-genre novel."
~Publishers Weekly

Please note that just like Dark-Hunter, the books don't have to be read in order. Sherrilyn always takes care to make sure that new readers won't be lost, no matter where they come in.

The League series is divided into three distinct timelines. Nemesis Rising® which is about Nemesis (Nykyrian) rising up against the League and the war that ensues between the League and his rival organization, the Sentella. And then later, Nemesis Legacy® that takes place decades after the war ends and involves many of the children of the original Sentella members. Nemesis Dynasty™ is a trilogy about Talyn Batur as he rises from the streets on Andaria to become the first Andarion Ring fighter in history to move from the Open to the Vested leagues, and changes Andarion politics forever.

Nemesis

The League® is an interstellar political drama that revolves around the central character, Nykyrian Quiakides. H
human, half-Andation, he was born too human to be accepted by his Andarion grandmother who cast him out and
Andarion to be accepted by humans. Forced into a human orphanage, he was adopted by a League commander
didn't want a son as much as he wanted a weapon he could train. A legend he could groom.

Nykyrian quickly became the very thing the commander wanted, and one of the deadliest assassins in
League's history.

Until the day came when he was asked to kill the one thing he couldn't.

A mother who actually loved and protected her child.

Instead, he did the unthinkable. He went rogue and started his own rival organization to the League. A grou
assassins dedicated to protecting the innocent targeted by the League and others to make sure that they are k
safe in a universe where every life has a price.

Darling Cruel

When we first meet Darling. he is a man of many secrets who rises from prince to emperor of the Caronese Empire. He is also the demolition expert for the Sentella, and has a bit of an anger management issue, which tends to be a bit of a problem for someone who likes to play with explosives for a hobby. Needless to say, it's always interesting whenever Darling enters a scene.

But then what do you expect from someone whose personal motto is: Da nullam clementiam – give no mercy. And whose codename is Kere, the Caronese god of death.

Nykyrian, Darling and Syn are three of Sherri's oldest characters. They were actually her imaginary playmates when she was a small child in elementary school.

Jayne Toole Erixour

One of Nykyrian's oldest "friends" and a distant cousin, Jayne is also the first member to join him for his Sentella crew. The daughter of an infamous thief and scoundrel, she grew up running scams and angles with her dad. He wasn't exactly a model parent. Yet Jayne was always loyal to him, even after he was sent to prison.

Which was how she became an assassin. After her father's sentence, her sister Eve took her in and trained her to be part of her team of freelance assassins who take missions to hunt hefty bounties.

And it was on just such a mission that Jayne met Hadrian, which is a whole other story.

Operating under the codename Shinikuri,(death-stalker), she is relentless once she takes a target.

Both Jayne and Eve had military SF short stories that Sherri sold in the 1980s to a number of science fiction magazines in a series Sherri called Eve of Destruction. Back then, Sherri wrote the stories under the pseudonym Alex Woodward and Kyle Hunter. They were so popular that the editor of a popular SF publisher asked her to submit a novel for them to him. When she did, Sherri made the mistake of putting her real name on them. The editor took one look at "Sherrilyn" and dismissed the science fiction manuscript out of hand by saying that they didn't publish "women's fiction" and that Sherri should send it to another imprint at their house.

Jayne Erixour
Active Duty
Rank: High Command
Species: Hyshian
Branch: Assassin
Alliance Forces
Sentella Command

C.I. Syn

The last to officially join the Sentella ranks is the one Nykyrian owes the most to. Sheridan Wade AKA C. I. Syn. The son of one of the most notorious criminals in the Ichidian universe and in its history. His father was so evil, that he is judged for his father's crimes. A convicted felon himself, Syn tried to hide his past and rebuild his life as a respected doctor with Nykyrian's help after he saved Nykyrian's life.

For a time, it worked. But no one can ever hide from their past. Betrayed by his wife, he was forced back to the streets and there he returned to what he knew best. Cyber espionage and robotics He's the Sentella's techspert and he's the best ever born.

*Syn was originally named Rachol Verlaine in a weird homage to the song a **Boy Named Sue**, which was a favorite tune played by Sherri's father when she was a girl. When she created her character as a young girl and she envisioned a tough "street rat" who was hated by his own father, she couldn't think of a better way to toughen him up and help to make him mean and bitter at an early age. His name was changed later because of contractual issues with her publishers.*

Dancer Hauk

Another distant cousin of Nykyrian's, Hauk actually grew up as a close confidante to Nykyrian's fraternal twin brother and mortal enemy Jullien. But as we've learned in the first half of the series, no one is ever Jullien's friend for long. Because of Jullien, Hauk loses his place in the Andarion military and joins Nykyrian's rebel cause to protect those who are wrongfully persecuted. He is one of the Sentella's High Command and a key asset.

*In the 1980s, Hauk and Jayne's sister, Eve, had a fling. Luckily before publication, it dawned on Sherri how closely related they were, and she removed their relationship from the short story. Eve was then given Jinx Shadowborn and Sumi was created for Hauk. That published 1985 short story was called **Hi Jinx**.*

Hermione "Kirren" Dane

The leader of the Tavali Nation of pirates is no one's fool and neither is her son, Ryn. She is a fierce leader and protector of her people and she'll stop at nothing to see that the League doesn't infringe on the rights of others. Even though she had the chance to marry Darling's father and become the empress of the Caronese people, she refused because that would have meant losing her place with the Tavali, as well as losing her independence as a captain and a pirate. Two things she will never do.

It's a decision she has never regretted. Now, she is part of the Sentella Alliance and she and her people are at war against the League and they will stop at nothing to see Kyr stopped in his oppression. Not until everyone in the Ichidian universe can sleep in peace, and not fear his tyrannical madness.

Hermione takes her name from the daughter of Helen of Troy who was left behind after her mother was kidnaped. As a girl, Sherri was fascinated by the story and wrote the tale of what happened to Helen's daughter in fourth grade. That story is what spawned the character for Hermione Dane.

Jullien eton Anatole

Fraternal twin of Nykyrian, he was allowed to stay on Andaria because he looked Andarian enough to pass as one of them. But his life wasn't much better than Nykyrian's. For one thing, their mother and aunt never forgave him for the fact that is his brother was "dead" because of him. Nor did his grandmother ever let him forget that he was half-human and thus a disappointment from birth.

And once his family learns that Nykyrian is alive and well, Jullien is cast out from everything he's ever known and branded a traitor. Hunted and hated, he has no one he can depend on.

Until he's taken in by the Tavali.

Jullien's Tavali alias is Dagger Ixur and he makes a stunning reappearance in **Born of Fury**.

NYKYRIAN & JULLIEN

Ushara of the Fyreblood Clan Altaan

For the first time in *Born of Betrayal*, readers learn that there are different races of Andarions. Ushara is one of the rarest that was driven off planet when Catriona's (the current reigning queen) mother went on a genocide to purify their species and eradicate all except for the dominate race (which is why it was such a slap in the face that her own daughter chose to have the sons of a human).

Now part of the Gorturnum, she is Trajen's right hand and the Vice Admiral of her nation. She's also Jullien's wife and the one who has the unfortunate job of riding herd on him.

Ushara made her first real appearance in the 1981 short story, **Blood Fyre,** *and in the novel draft* **Cry of the Raven.**

Nemesis Rising

When Sherri first sat down to begin her series as a little girl in the 1970s, she never intended to skip ahead with it. Her original vision for the series was to write Nyrkyrian's rise from an orphan to the strongest League assassin, to emperor and then to his retirement where his sons and daughter took over.

But as John Lennon once said, life is what happens while you're making other plans. And though she'd written and published a number of short stories in the eighties, what she couldn't foresee was the death of her elder brother right as she finished typing out the draft of *Born of Night* in 1987 on a typewriter she borrowed from him. Buddy wasn't just her brother, he was her biggest supporter and best friend. Anyone who's read the prologue knows how much he meant to her and how much his loss took her under.

To this day, she mourns him.

It was during the eighties that Sherrilyn would handwrite the first four novels of the League series: *Born of Night*. *Born of Fire*. *Born of Shadows* and *Born of Silence*. But because of the actions of her first husband and his insistence on negotiating her first contract even though she argued against his getting involved with her career, he ended up angering her editor and causing *Born of Night* to be delayed a full six years from coming out (the full contractual length that the editor could delay it without the publisher losing rights to the book). More than that, because of his actions, her then husband caused her to be black-balled in the industry.

It was a hard blow for a young writer (Sherri was just twenty-four when she first sold the series). And it tied-up the rights for The League books for sixteen years 1991-2007). The editor was so angry, that she kept the option books, Born of Fire and Born Shadows tied up for over two years before she finally refused them.

Which meant Sherri couldn't do anything, at all, with the League books while she waited to hear back from her editor who was furious with her because of what her husband had done.

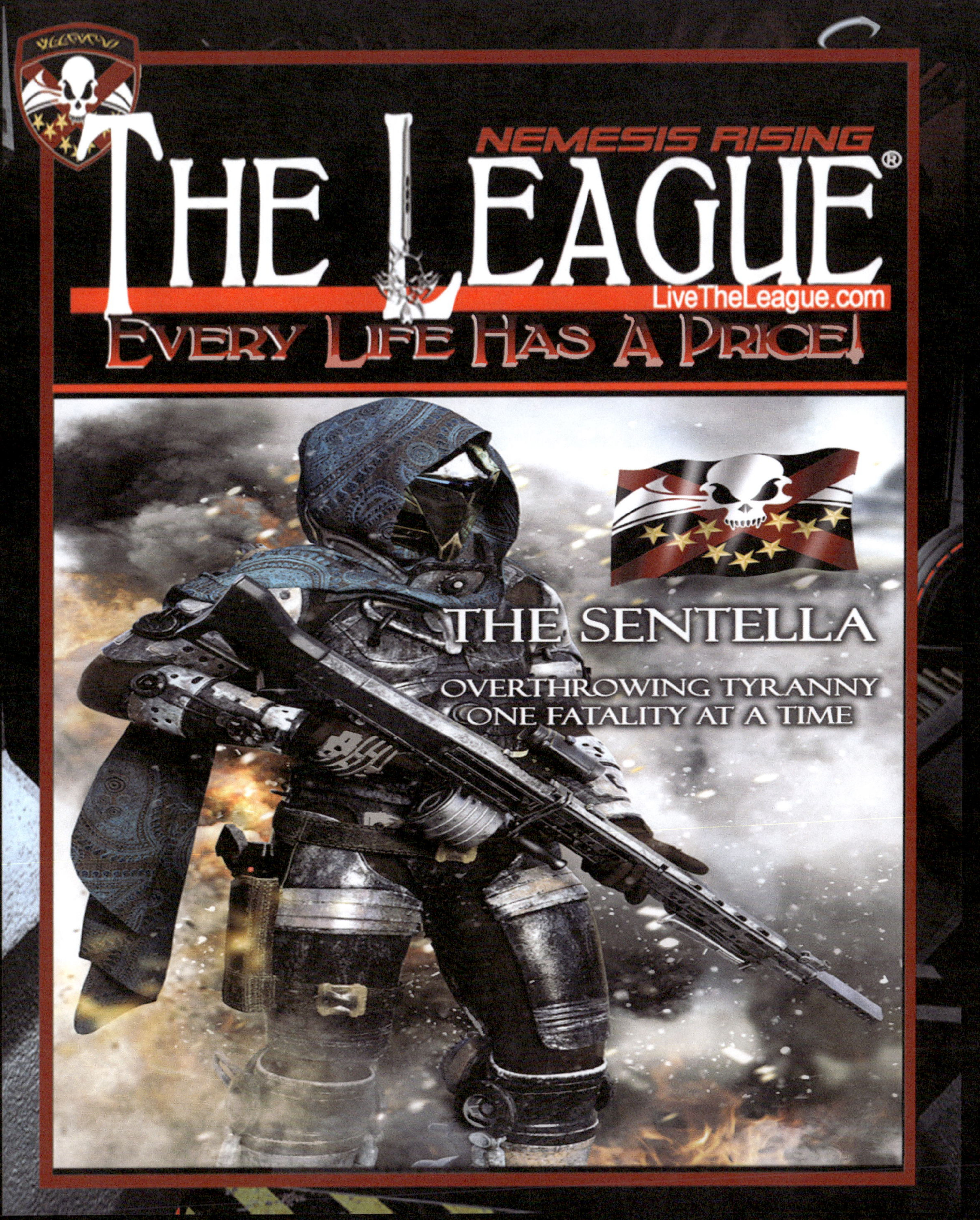

NEMESIS RISING
THE LEAGUE®
LiveTheLeague.com
EVERY LIFE HAS A PRICE!
THE SENTELLA
OVERTHROWING TYRANNY
ONE FATALITY AT A TIME

OMG
Gouran, Gourish
Gouran Consulate

Kiara Biardi - Amber eyes, dk brown
Nykiyrian Quiatides - Blue eyes, Blond
Arostrion - Blond hair
Com. Kiarun Biardi
Serela
Dancer Hauk - Blk hair / Red + wt eyes
Jayne Diarc - Sharp features / Blk hair
Rachel Verlaine - ass, contrac
Darling Cruel - Dk. Auburn / Blue -
Arturo
Caillen Dagan
Shahara Dagan
Kasen Dagan
Mira - plump - short
Chenzira
Petiri
Emp. Abenbi - Pro.

Rachel Verlaine
Shahara Dagan

Chrysla - Shahara's
Blaise

Diano - weapon thate,

Skoa gens - scent

BOOK

Dec '74

GLUED CONSTRUCTION

NAME Sherri Woodward

100 SHEETS 9-5/8 IN. X 7-1/2 IN. 5950/100

Union Camp

Circe Alyssa   D'iya Briola   Blond/Green   ship
(Siroun) Caillen Dagan - dk ht eyes
Gevork Vartan - Caillen's Father   Sakerian Empire   45005
Gt Magar - Krikorian soldier   seladen - hors
Krikor - Gevork's planet
                                   Adion - Eunis
Duinan Hauk - Dancer's Brother
Alonst - Alyssa's maid
Eyup - minor character in chapt 1
Teca - Caillen's mother
Kamaria - Alyx's

Nemesis Legacy

But Sherri is nothing if not resilient. With her rights tied up because of her husband's shenanigans and her editor refusing to give her an answer on her option books, she returned to the partials and notes she'd made in middle and high school for her series. Since she'd planned all along to continue the series past the parents to their kids, Sherri decided to skip ahead to the next generation.

Yet that wasn't going to be as easy as it seemed. For one thing, she didn't want to put spoilers in the Legacy books about their parents. And two, there was a pesky little thing called a non-compete clause in her publishing contract that her agent warned her about.

Non-compete, what?

Non-compete clause. That meant that everything Sherrilyn had created in the series (characters, planets, languages, governments, etc.) had to be renamed to something else. Everything. That was how Rachol Verlaine became C.I. Syn. No character could be left standing.

Not even the League. It ended up being renamed the Omniumgatherum (OMG), because Sherri had no idea in 1991 that years later the internet would be booming and OMG would become a thing (or that Amazon would come along and invent its own Alexa that she had in her books, too). Come to think of it, Mom had a lot of things that have since become reality.

Anyway, no sooner had Sherrilyn finished Paradise City, the book about Syn or Rachol's son than it sold to a different publisher. And though it was her third book that she sold, it ended up coming out first—yeah, publishing can be a weird animal sometimes.

Which explains why when Sherri handed in the option book about Adron (the book that was originally titled *Born of Ice*) after Devyn, the publisher decided they didn't want another SF from Sherrilyn because they'd heard the rumors from Sherri's other editor, and so ended the League Legacy books at a second publishing house, tying up the rights for a different branch of the series for another sixteen years . . .

Born of Fire

Adversity is no stranger to Sherrilyn. Over, under, around or through is her personal motto. Undaunted by the challenges being thrown at her, she relentlessly moved forward, ever determined to prove her critics wrong. Even though her first novel, *Paradise City*, was the first book in RT history to get a one star rating.

It's true. Up until she published her first book, their lowest rating was only three stars. But as luck would have it, they decided to drop it down to a one star system the very month her first book came out and she was the lucky recipient. But the thing about Mom, she's glad it was her and not someone else.

Still, it hurt. But she took her lump and kept going.

This was 1995, the year I was born and a new thing had just started . . . electronic books. Being a trendsetter and a technophile, Mom was instantly intrigued. She believed in the future and since publishers back then didn't think e-books would ever take off, they hadn't started grabbing the rights for them.

Which meant Sherrilyn was free to take her series into a new format. Taking a deep breath, she went in and contacted one of the burgeoning new companies, Dreams Unlimited and pitched them her old book, *Born of Fire*.

They accepted and Sherri became the first traditional "New York" published author to put out an e-book. Ironically, DU also signed another of Sherri's books, an unknown book about Daimons called, *Night Pleasures*, but sadly they went out of business before the could publish Kyrian's book.

Ichidian Universe National Flags
LiveTheLeague.com

THE UNITED SYSTEMS

THE LEAGUE

THE OVERSEER

ANDARIA BATTLE FLAG

ANDARIA PEACE FLAG

CARON

EXETER

GONDARA

GOURAN

HYSHA

PHRIXUS

PROBEKA

QILLA

RITADARIA

TONDARA

TRIOSA

TRISA

ULTARIA

Ichidian Universe Rebel Flags
LiveTheLeague.com

SENTELLA

KIMMERIAN

TAVALI UNIVERSAL

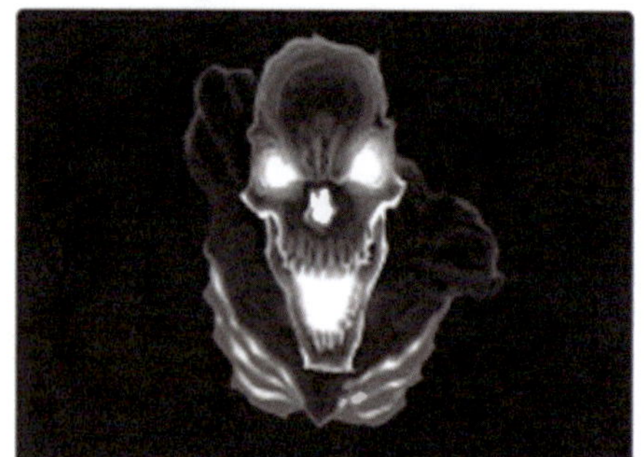

TAVALI GORTURNUM

TAVALI WASTURNUM

TAVALI SEPTURNUM

TAVALI PORTURNUM

TAVALI – RYN

TAVALI – FAIN

TAVALI -- CHAYDEN

TAVALI – STARLA

TAVALI -- TARYN

Fire & Ice

Years after Sherrilyn's publisher turned down Adron's book and after another hundred rejections for it (we're not exaggerating), Sherri finally had an offer from Berkley for an anthology. She was thrilled!

Until she got the call from the editor letting her know that one of the authors on the project refused to be in the anthology so long as Sherri was in it (the author didn't want to share her readers with Sherrilyn). Since Berkley was courting this author to bring her over to their house, they naturally couldn't allow Sherri to be in the anthology and moved her out of it, even though Sherri really needed the money to help pay for an operation for our brother (she was just getting off welfare and was still getting back on her feet from being homeless with me).

It was really hard times,

But ever optimistic, Mom dug out her old novel and began cutting it down for the new anthology theme. While it wasn't the novel she'd originally written, it was enough to keep the series alive until she could get the rights back.

Number 1

In 2009, eighteen years after the first book sold, and after all the ups and downs, trials and tribulations, Sherrilyn finally placed the first three books of the League series at Number 1. She's the only woman to place a science fiction series at #1 on the *New York Times* without having a movie tie-in for it, and she's done it multiple times.

Her fans can't seem to get enough. That being said, there was a small interruption in the publishing schedule when Sherri moved the League from St. Martin's to another publisher because SMP wanted to put more time between them to keep attention on the Dark-Hunters.

Sadly, the publisher Sherri moved them to was extremely heavy-handed and after the editor actually went in and rewrote entire paragraphs of her novels, she decided to buy back the third novel and return them to St. Martin's.

Everything was going well with the series and Sherri was again on track when out of the blue her ex-husband derailed the League schedule with an unexpected divorce that caused her books to be delayed.

Now caught in the middle of an unrelenting nightmare, Sherrilyn is fighting for her worlds, characters and series that she started long before she met her ex who did his best to keep her from writing and pursuing her dreams. The very same person who is still getting in the way of her publishing her books and moving on with her life.

League Young Adult

Long before Sherri wrote the adult books, she first started writing a young adult version of the League books. As she grew older, those original stories developed into a trilogy that became League Dynasty.

Centered around Talyn Batur (the illegitimate son of Fain Hauk), the books chronicle his journey from a troubled teen who is struggling to care for his mother to his becoming a champion ring fighter.

Working with Kevin J. Anderson, Sherrilyn was on the brink of turning her high school stories and concepts into novels when again her ex intervened and caused the project to be put on hold for the time being. Hopefully, one day soon Sherri's old stories will be told

Andarion

Sherri has invented an entire working language for her Andarion race, as well as Caronese, Trisani, Ritadarion, etc. They have their own grammar books, and vocabulary sheets. She's also set up their histories and has mapped the entire Ichidian universe.

She takes her world building very seriously.

THE RING LEADER
SPLATTERDOME

EXCLUSIVE!
THE IRON HAMMER
FINALLY SPEAKS

UNDEFEATED!
FROM OPEN TO VESTED
TALYN BATUR DOES
THE IMPOSSIBLE

LIVETHELEAGUE.COM

League Religions

Each character also has his or her own religious beliefs, and they don't always agree. Jullien is even adopted by a high priestess of an Andarion religion (Demurist) that was banned by his Azukarian grandmother.

Some are monotheistic, some polytheistic, agnostic and others are atheist. Just like you'd find on earth. Every character is different. It's what makes the world feel so real and the characters live and breathe.

Tavali

During the Scythian Age when the greedy warlords were at their worst, the Nation was the creation of Lemuel Snitch and his First Lady Verily. Known free traders, and independent operators, and defenders of freedom, they defied the corrupt governments and fought to keep the wormholes and space lanes open for honest tradesmen who were sick of being taxed, jailed, over regulated, and abused by governments out to line their pockets through robbery and treachery.

Back then, it was nothing for cargo and trade ships to be seized any time they crossed into uncharted areas of space, or even into well-known trade lanes by shady officials who made trumped up regulation violation allegations and espionage charges against them. Ships and cargo were routinely impounded and sold for no reason whatsoever. Crews were seized and imprisoned, even sold and executed, often without due process.

After the death of their youngest daughter, Tavali, and her crew at the hands of the Krellans over trumped up allegations of spying and smuggling (she was making a humanitarian run through their territory under a missionary's plague banner and had the correct paperwork and permits), Lemuel and Verily rallied their colleagues to form their own coalition of tradesmen who would protect each other. A brotherhood of independent owners, runners, freighters, and any pilot who didn't want to be bound to a government out to rule them with a tyrannical fist, but rather be left to make a living on their own terms. They would become their own protectors and form an alliance guild so strong that the other governments would be forced to recognize their worker coalition, and let them trade in peace and safety. To negotiate with them as real traders and not take advantage of the fact that they were independents.

Originally called the Tavalian League in honor of Tavali Snitch, they flew under a single, plain black flag of grief to pay tribute to, and as a reminder of, the brave and noble men and women who'd died alone without the rights they now bonded together to protect.

Once word spread of their brotherhood guild and objectives, and they solidified and ratified the Tavalian Code and Council, their numbers grew quickly.

TNT 'Cock' Patch
Gorturnum Nation

Trajen Scalera

Very little is known about Trajen Dane Thaumarturgus. He came into the Tavali as a teenager under the reign and adoption of Travelyan Dane (the father of Hermione "Kirren" Dane) and quickly rose to the rank of Tavali commander. Turning Rogue immediately, he left the Wasternum nation, and in one of the bloodiest takeovers in Tavali history, he defeated Valden DaVers in the Calibrim for the rank of High Admiral & Presidium of the Gorturnum nation.

Since then, he's lived more as a phantom and myth. Most only deal with his commanders. If you come under his attention, you don't live long enough to regret your blunder. The only things sharper than the strange Andarion warsword he carries are his witticisms and battle skills.

Maris & Darling

Long before it was the "in" thing, Sherri had an inclusive cast of characters. Her League series had openly gay characters back in the early 1980s and when the first novel was published, she was required to downplay them and remove Maris from the earlier books.

She also took a lot of heat from the fact that Darling was only pretending to be gay, but that was the crux of both his and Maris's relationship from the beginning. That they were both two sides of a complicated relationship. Darling was straight pretending to be gay and Maris was gay pretending to be straight, both helping the other to pass himself off in a society that didn't accept him so that he wouldn't be "outed" for it. Both trying their best to be someone they're not in order to protect the people they love.

Each character showing how hard it is to hide your true feelings and to pretend, even when your life, and that of your family, is at stake.

Sherrilyn Woodward McQueen

And just like the characters and worlds she creates, Sherri will continue to rise to the challenges that life throws at her. One of her favorite quotes comes from her Uncle Carlos: our family doesn't run. Sometimes we might want to. Sometimes we probably ought to. But we don't ever run.

That is, at her core, our mother. She is every bit the warrior her father was. Whether she's Kyle Hunter, Cherice Moon, Alex Woodward, Sherrilyn Woodward, Sherrilyn Kenyon or now Sherrilyn McQueen, she's always a fighter who loves her sons, her family, her worlds and her fans.

She will stand strong and fight for us all.

The one thing you can always count on is that she doesn't look back. She only looks to the future. Armed with a new name, she won't let her past define her or weigh her down.

After all, there's a brave new world out there and she's dying to discover it. Mom is nothing if not intrepid. That's why we love her.

Silent Swans

One of the future projects Sherri is hoping to get to is one that has been back-burnered due to her ex's unconscionable acts over the last few years. Originally slated to come out in 2015, the Silent Swans are a trilogy of books based on Sherrilyn's great-great-grandmothers who helped to build America.

These weren't meek and mild women. They were movers and shakers who rose up and carved for themselves and their children a better tomorrow and who left a lasting legacy that we feel to this day. Each book will chronicle the life of a little known heroine who made a major contribution to American history.

2
THE DARK-HUNTERS: INFINITY
SHERRILYN KENYON
ART BY JIYOUNG AHN

the DARK HUNTERS
1 volume
Story by Sherrilyn Kenyon
Art by Claudia Campos

the DARK HUNTERS

New York Times Bestselling
the DARK HUNTERS

LORDS OF AVALON
KNIGHT OF DARKNESS
MARVEL
SHERRILYN KENYON
TOMMY OHTSUKA
ROBIN FURTH

3 volume
Story by Sherrilyn Kenyon
Art by Claudia Campos

New York Times Bestselling
the DARK HUNTERS
4 volume
Story by Sherrilyn Kenyon
Art by Claudia Campos

Past, Present, Future

As noted, the Silent Swans aren't Sherri's only historical venture. Her worlds have included every type of setting and genre: contemporary, horror, science fiction, mystery, young adult, comics . . . There's nothing she hasn't claimed as her own and made her mark in.

Sherrilyn has always believed in going wherever her muse carries her. We're grateful for that.

Knowing her mind, we can only imagine where she'll take us from here, but one thing we know, she never leaves a world behind. So for all those waiting for stories, rest assured that she has something brewing.

They are, after all, her babies, and she loves all her babies.

New Worlds

And if you've ever wondered, my mom says that she has entire worlds that have been in her head since childhood that she has yet to begin writing about. That if she never had another idea again, she has more than enough to carry her for the next hundred years.

Our job is to bury her with a laptop and a really long extension cord so that she can 1) nag us from the grave to clean our rooms and 2) continue to "ghost" write her stories.

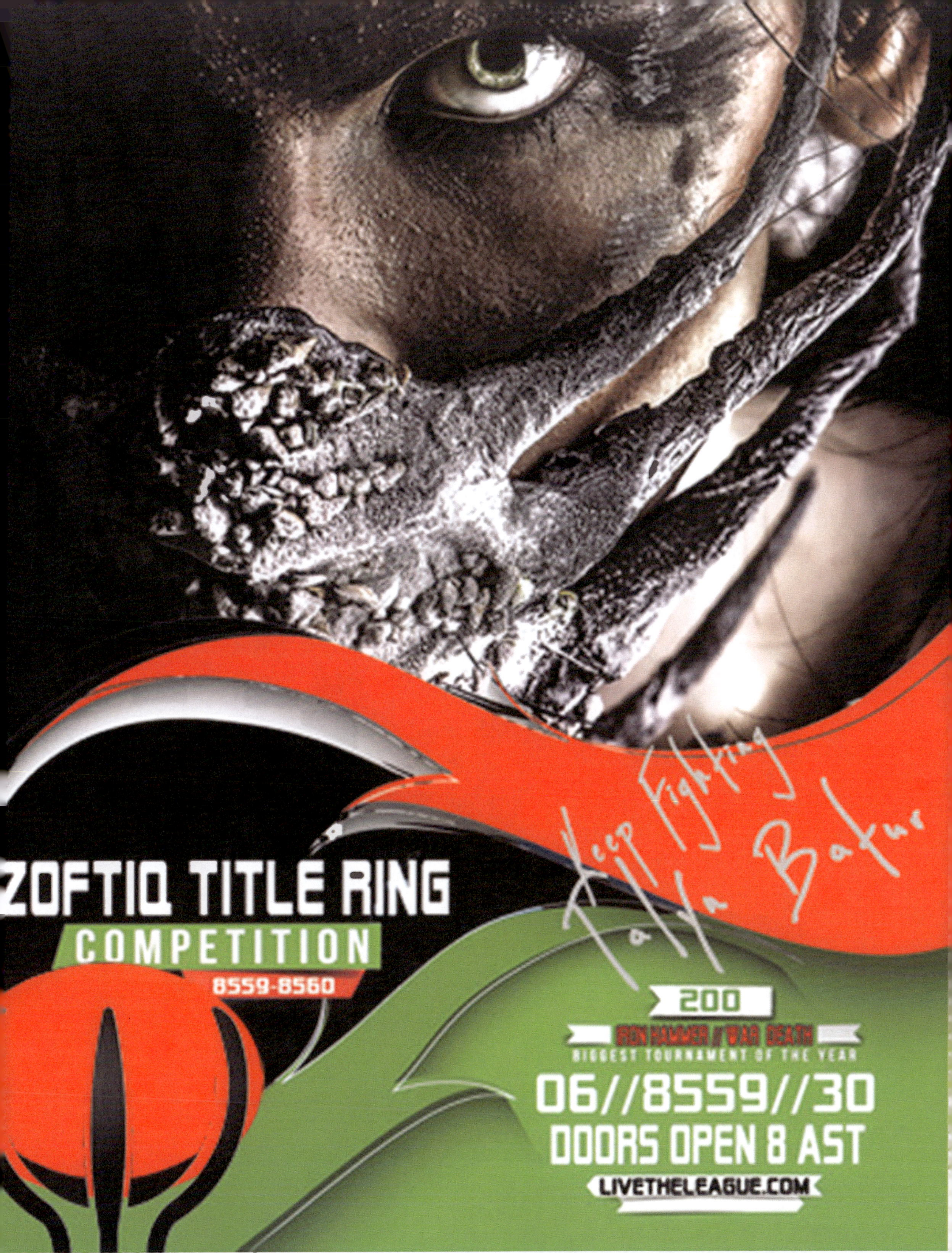
ZOFTIQ TITLE RING
COMPETITION
8559-8560
200
IRON HAMMER // WAR DEATH
BIGGEST TOURNAMENT OF THE YEAR
06//8559//30
DOORS OPEN 8 AST
LIVETHELEAGUE.COM

Until Then . . .

Enjoy these last few looks at her characters as captured by Sherrilyn and the Dabel Brothers. As Mom would say, upwards and onwards. There's a lot to do and not a lot of time to do it. We'll be seeing you soon!

FAIN HAUK
ACTIVE DUTY

RANK:
ADJUTANT
SPECIES:
ANDARION
BRANCH:
ARMADA

TALYN BATUR
ACTIVE DUTY

RANK:
LT. COMMANDER
SPECIES:
ANDARION
BRANCH:
ARMADA

ALLIANCE FORCES
SENTELLA COMMAND

NYKYRIAN QUIAKIDES
ACTIVE DUTY

RANK:
HIGH COMMAND
SPECIES:
HYBRID
BRANCH:
TECH/ASSASSIN

DARLING CRUEL
ACTIVE DUTY

RANK:
HIGH COMMAND
SPECIES:
HUMAN
BRANCH:
TECH

MORRA
CHEHO'VITASTAMIUTSTOH
(WE CAN'T PRONOUNCE IT EITHER)
ACTIVE DUTY

RANK:
COLONEL
SPECIES:
SCHVARDAN
BRANCH:
ASSASSIN

ALLIANCE FORCES
SENTELLA COMMAND

IN A UNIVERSE WHERE THE LEAGUE IS LAW, MOST LIVE IN FEAR . . .

WE FIGHT BACK

LIVETHELEAGUE.COM

XANS-SULLE
MARIS

MARIS XANS-SULLE OF PHRIXUS

CASTE:
IMMIGRANT

TITLE:
AMBASSADOR

ADDRESS:
6799 COURT OF ANDARIA
ERIS, ANATOLE V62S235

BEFORE YOU RATTLE MY CAGE, YOU BETTER MAKE SURE I'M PADLOCKED IN IT.

~FELICIA

BBQ!

In Lov
Memory

www.dark-hunter.com | www.dabelbrothers.com

THE END IS NEAR

Intense gamer, former teacher and current mastermind of all around mayhem, Madaug Kenyon first started writing in grade school . . . on his mother's walls. Deciding that near death experiences weren't exactly his forte, he traded his crayons for a computer, and once he broke away from his severe gaming addiction, realized that his keyboard could also be used to create his own worlds. He's been doing that ever since. The author of his own online intergalactic comic, Space Sovereign, he's currently at work finishing his second novel.

Ian Kenyon didn't want to follow in his family footsteps. He did everything he could not to be a writer. But those pesky characters wouldn't leave him alone. Deciding that he was either a writer or schizophrenic, he finally sat down and began putting the voices in his head on paper. Grateful to learn that once he put them there, they left his head, he realized that he had no choice, except to admit defeat. He was a writer and his characters had won. Now he's working on getting his first book published while running his own trading card company, The Black Hat Society, LLC. A company MUCH different from the books his mother writes!

Defying all odds is what #1 New York Times and international bestselling author Sherrilyn Kenyon does best. Rising from extreme poverty as a child that culminated in being a homeless mother with an infant, she has become one of the most popular and influential authors in the world (in both adult and young adult fiction), with dedicated legions of fans known as Paladins–thousands of whom proudly sport tattoos from her numerous genre-defying series.

Since her first book debuted in 1993 while she was still in college, she has placed more than 80 novels on the New York Times list in all formats and genres, including manga and graphic novels, and has more than 70 million books in print worldwide. Her current series include: Dark-Hunters®, Chronicles of Nick®, Deadman's Cross™, Black Hat Society™, Nevermore™, Silent Swans™, Lords of Avalon® and The League®.

Join her and her Paladins online at QueenofAllShadows.com and www.facebook.com/mysherrilyn.